Ty

2⁰⁰

Home at Last

Home at Last

Jean McGarry

The Johns Hopkins University Press
Baltimore and London

This book has been brought to publication with the generous assistance of the G. Harry Pouder Fund.

The Johns Hopkins University Press
2715 North Charles Street
Baltimore, Maryland 21218-4319
The Johns Hopkins Press Ltd., London

Acknowledgment is made to the editors of *Southwest Review* for two stories that first appeared in slightly different form in their pages: "Every Hour That Goes By Grows Younger" and "The Sacrifice"; to the *New Yorker* for "Sex-Linked Traits"; *North American Review* for "Mr. and Mrs. Bull" (originally "Ozark Winter"); *Southern Review* for "Uncle Maggot"; and *Yale Review* for "The Raft."

Library of Congress Cataloging-in-Publication Data will be found at the end of this book.

A catalog record for this book is available from the British Library.

For Deborah M. and Frank T. McGarry

Contents

I

The Raft

First his father died by falling out of a window in his feathered hat. It was on Memorial Day, 1938. They had driven the red geranium to the cemetery, knelt in front of the family tombstone, and while his father prayed, or at least shut his eyes tight, Jimmy read the names of people from the family who were already under the stone: four McGinnises—Great Auntie Alice, who lived in Pawtucket; Uncle Joe McGinnis, who was run over by a streetcar; Grandfather Henry J. McGinnis, who died up at the state institution after living there for twenty years, and Grandmother Mary McGinnis, whom Jimmy couldn't remember because she had died when he was a baby. His father knelt on the bag the flowers had come in, and Jimmy knelt beside him. The grass was soft and damp and it wet his trouser knees. His mother had made him wear his blue suit with long pants. Later on, she said, you can wear your sailor suit for the parade. It was on Memorial Day that people switched to their whites: white shoes, white stockings, white dresses, and white hats. You wore white until Labor Day, she said, then went back to what people normally wore: black or brown; when winter came, it was all black coats and black hats. His mother wore a brown feather to dress up her good black hat, a long thin feather, speckled with white. It was this kind of feather, his mother told him, that people dipped in ink; they sharpened the point with a knife and wrote their letters. His father said this *wasn't* the kind of feather they used—it wasn't at all this kind of feather! But his mother and father always disagreed; they couldn't agree on anything.

His father had gone out and bought a red plant for 25 cents. On Memorial Day, they sold geraniums everywhere, and as you got close to the cemetery, they were on every street corner. Jimmy didn't like the smell, but they last, his mother said, and you don't have to water them. In the old days, she told him, people would break the pot against the gravestone and plant the flower right in the soft earth. And there it would grow until the next year, when out it would come, and in would go a new one. Times change, she said; no one would think of doing a thing like that now.

When they came back from the cemetery after laying the flower with the McGinnises, his mother was ready with a big Sunday breakfast. Conversation at the table was all about the parade, where his father would wear the full regalia of the presiding Knight of Columbus: black cutaway and black pants, a cape with a white satin lining and a stiff black hat with plumes. Jimmy wanted to help him buckle on the sword but his father said no, he would dress at the post, where they kept the uniforms. His mother said that maybe Jimmy could come along? No, his father said, there were no children allowed on this day or any day, subject closed.

Removing the eggy plates, his mother remarked, "I don't know what's gotten into your father. And him that was always such an easy man to live with." Jimmy looked at his father and waited for the explosion, but that day there was no explosion. His father finished with his tea, wiped his mouth on the checked napkin, and left the table. And that year's parade was no different from all the others: his father led the rows of marching Knights and looked neither left nor right. Jimmy's mother set up her canvas chair in front of the barber shop, and there she sat when the soldiers marched by, the army trucks and jeeps, the even rows of drum and fife. She got up to look at the Girl Scouts and the Legion of Mary, all in blue with ribbons around their necks; the Knights, the floats, and the baton twirlers. She sat down again for the lines of veterans from the war.

The parade that year was normal, but nothing else was. Jimmy was ten years old, but there was no birthday party. There was no extra money for party favors, balloons, and bubbles, or for cake and ice cream. But he had had a party the year before, his mother reminded him, and wasn't *that* a swell time! Ten guests, pink cake with blocks of vanilla ice cream, pin the tail on the donkey, musical chairs. For his tenth birthday, she cooked his favorite supper, and he was lucky, she said, to get that. His father's business had gone broke after the first of the year. It was a business begun by the grandfather and great-uncle in 1885, and all the trucks—the cement mixer, the dump trucks, and the one panel truck—said MCGINNIS & MCGINNIS CEMENT— —FOUNDED 1885.

Right after it happened, his father came home every night restless and silent. Once, when his mother thought the father was barricaded in his bedroom with the door shut tight, she told Jimmy that someone had had a hand in the till. His father overheard it and he exploded: "Jesus, Mary, and Joseph!" they heard coming from the bedroom. "Don't let me ever hear you say that again!" He came into the kitchen, his face dark red and circles under his eyes—"Or I'll kill you dead!"

"Don't you speak to me that way, Mister!" his mother shot back. "And in front of the boy!" She was holding Jimmy against her, hands on his shoulders, but the father didn't come near them. He sat down at the kitchen table and Jimmy fled the room. Later on, he could hear the sound of his father crying and choking, and his mother's soothing voice—the voice she had also used on him when a playmate broke his clipper ship with the real cloth sails, or when the nuns punished him for wearing a white shirt that was too yellow. After a while his father marched out of the house. Jimmy heard the door slam and feet pounding down the steps. He went to the window and saw the black car, washed and waxed every Sunday, rolling over the gravel and into the street, and then his father was gone. He waited in his room. First he heard the sound of the kettle screaming on the stove and then the stifled sound of his mother weeping, as she sometimes did, in the broom closet, her face buried in a clump of dusters. He ran out of his room and nuzzled his head in her side, bumpy with corset bones. He wrapped his arms around her waist and worked himself up until his sobs were louder than hers, and then she pulled him out of the closet, dragged him to a kitchen chair, and sat him down on her lap. She wiped his face with a duster. When he was finished crying, she invited him to take a cup of tea with her and catch his breath. They were at the beginning of "the crisis."

Throughout the winter and spring, he heard how *no one* had had a hand in the till. The blame lay elsewhere. Times were hard, the Depression was on, and nobody needed a new sidewalk or had the money to pay for it. Not even the city—where most of their contracts came from, thanks to Uncle Henry who got out the vote every four years—could afford a new sidewalk. And with City Hall broke and defenseless, the muckrakers were beginning to dig out the dirt. McGinnis & McGinnis, his mother told him, was high on the list of builders improperly hired. They had read headlines in the papers: corruption, it said, favoritism, kickbacks, sweetheart contracts. And for a while, there was nothing coming in to pay the rent or the bill for sand. "Your dada isn't bringing home enough," his mother said, "to feed a family of ants," and his father exploded again.

But somehow they weathered it, "the crisis." Uncle Henry, it turned out, had a nest egg and his father borrowed on it. Business picked up again, mostly federal projects and work for people whose money was in solid assets. And his father was going to save a bundle renting their beach house for the summer, except for the week in June when he had reserved it for them. They were going to set out the day after Memorial Day. His mother had done a week's worth of cooking and baking. Once on the shore, she told him, she planned to do nothing but sit on the piazza and let the good times roll. It had been a hard winter, they had survived, and she had a good rest coming to her.

But of course they never went, and he was sure that he'd never see that beach house again. Instead of packing the car after the parade, they were standing around in the parlor with neighbors and relations and some people Jimmy didn't know. His Uncle Henry had driven Jimmy home from the parade, speeding on the city streets, bouncing in and out of potholes. Jimmy hid his head in the rough upholstery and now his face felt itchy. He licked his lips and tasted salt. People told him to be a good boy and be brave, and they forced him to eat things. His aunt handed him a slice of white bread with oleo and sugar on it. He had never seen a sandwich like that, but she said to eat it anyway. He held it up to his mouth and gagged. Someone snatched it away and told the aunt to leave the boy alone. Then Uncle Frank handed Jimmy his man's handkerchief with initials, FXM, and Jimmy put the cool cloth on his face. It was still Memorial Day, a day that seemed to last forever.

By then, they had taken his mother away to Aunt Mary's house. Jimmy went to stay with his cousins, but one day his Aunt Mary came for him, and drove him to her house. His mother was there, dressed in a bathrobe he had never seen before, blue stripes and very roomy. She was sitting by herself, looking out the window at the park across the street. She kept asking him to take a look and see if he could name all the beautiful trees, but he stayed put in his chair. It was a wonderful park, she said, and when the wind whistled, the little birdies sang. Aunt Mary was holding her hand, but his mother kept pulling it back. "How does my hair look?" she asked, and he knew enough not to say it looked a wreck, all matted and stringy—she hadn't even thought to braid it. Aunt Mary sat down on the bed and stroked the long hair, but his mother, it was clear, did not want to be touched. She wanted to be left in peace. She asked him again: "Sonny, my Sonny Boy, how is my Sonny Boy?" and he said fine.

On the way to the cousins', driving slowly through the park so Jimmy could see it really was beautiful and not just a story, Aunt Mary said that his mother was lucky to be out of the fray. Jimmy knew what she meant, but he didn't say anything: he listened. He knew the part about his father marching in the parade only to meet up with the state marshal, who told him to report directly to the police station. He didn't know why his father had to report, but he knew it was trouble. Someone said they didn't want to "manacle" him in front of the world. "Manacle" meant arrest, someone else said; it didn't mean shoot.

And his father was on his way back to the post, Aunt Mary said, when it happened. But she was wrong about this. His father never went back to the post. He drove to the Westminster Building and took the elevator up to the top and then he "sailed"—that's the word they used—out the ninth floor window. He was wearing his fancy dress suit, "highest order of Knight." He even had the feather hat on. The papers said that it blew up the street and landed in front of the Mr. Peanut store, which had a real Mr. Peanut right in the window. The hat was on the sidewalk.

But Jimmy didn't remember seeing the hat, and he had been there. He had met his father on the parade ground, accidentally on purpose, so he could get a ride to the post and see the Knights in costume, drinking beer and highballs. The first thing he noticed was his father was mad, but he expected that. "It serves you right, goddamn pest!" he said. "You pushed your way into this. You and your mother." It was a mouthful for him. He said it, and then they drove in silence to the Westminster Building, and then up in the elevator. His father said, "Sonny, you stay here and in five minutes, I want you to pick up the telephone and call the operator." His father was out of breath and sat down. He fumbled in his pocket and handed Jimmy a newly minted quarter, 1938. That was all he had in his pocket, he said; the rest of his gear was at the post. He looked at Jimmy and said, "Give your old man a hug, or don't you want to?" Then he walked into the old front office of McGinnis & McGinnis (the name on the door had been whitewashed, but you could still see it) with the key he kept. Hanging from the doorknob was a wooden sign on a string: Wm Franklin NOTARY PUBLIC. His father closed the door behind him.

"What happens to a person that falls?" Jimmy wanted to ask during the wake, but didn't have to because Mrs. Gavin, their neighbor, was herself asking Father Corcoran. The priest put on a long face and refused to answer. Then someone said, "Hey, that's the boy over there. He's listening." The priest's face turned dark red and he left the room. Someone else explained it. "Gravity," the man said, using a hand to demonstrate, "makes them get heavier as they fall." Jimmy waited, but the man didn't say more.

People told him a lot of things when he asked, but mostly he waited for someone else to ask, and then he listened to the answer. Some said that his father was sick and tired of living, he was in the hole, he was beside himself. Some said he showed no consideration whatsoever for his family; others said he showed too much. They said it was his fault, and that it wasn't his fault. They also said that if Jimmy prayed hard enough, his father wouldn't have to do much time in Purgatory. This was a lie. Jimmy went to parochial school and the nuns there said that taking your own life was always a mortal. There was no time to ask God's forgiveness, no time to make a fervent Act of Contrition. It meant his father was going to Hell. It was a permanent place and the nuns had told them exactly what it was like. "Go to Hell," Jimmy said to himself in his ugliest voice, but he still couldn't believe it.

Yet he was there when the judgment was made. The nuns said it took less than a minute, and by then the rescue squad had rolled up to the Westminster Building. Jimmy didn't even have to call them; they came on their own. The moment he heard the siren, he raced to the corridor. There was a window there and he could see it all. But it was only when they lifted his father off the sidewalk that he realized it was his father. At first he couldn't figure out how he'd gotten down there so fast.

After the rescue squad left, he didn't know what to do. He went down the elevator. He walked to the little park near City Hall where his father used to meet his cronies. He sat on a bench. He was too surprised to cry.

He wondered if anyone would ever find him, lost downtown. But Uncle Henry found him in no time. "Get in!" he yelled when he drove up. The streets were empty, just a few streamers and confetti left from the parade. By the time they got home, the cloudy sky had turned blue, just like his mother said it would. They should have told him, though, where she had gone because he began to search the house, and searched every single room from the parlor to the back porch, and when he found them all empty, he began to cry. His mother was alive, they all said. *She* wasn't the one, but it was her he kept calling for.

2

It was that same year when, walking home from school, the sky turned a brownish yellow and his mother was out on the sidewalk beating her arms against her sides, telling him to hurry. "Don't you see!" she yelled, when he was a block away, and then she took him by the shoulders and gave him a shaking—why had he dawdled on a day like this!—and hustled him up the stairs and into the house. There they waited, but at first there was nothing to hear: a few branches whistling in the wind and the screams of the starlings disturbed in the middle of the day. She made them a pot of tea and they drank it fortified with a tablespoon of whiskey. Then they heard it: the wind shrieking and rain beating on the parlor windows (she had pulled the shades and drawn the curtains, but they could still hear it). It was a Wednesday, a school day, but by three o'clock it was pitch dark and they had no electricity. She made him do his homework—arithmetic and a column of spelling words—by a candle whose flame blew first toward his face, then away from it. The house was full of drafts and sometimes a bolt of lightning would flash and the windows would whiten.

She tried to telephone the weather bureau, but the phone line was dead. They heard a sound—the wind roaring and a deafening crash— and she yelled to stay away from the goddamn windows so black, then all whitened again. The house trembled from the force of the crash and he crept over to the kitchen window, pulled away the lace curtain that had been sucked into the window hollow, and lifted a slat of the blind. At first he couldn't see anything but water rushing down, but then, for a minute, the rain hovered in the air and he saw that the huge oak tree in front of their house had fallen on the roof of the Petersons', and the McHenrys', too, who lived on the second floor. She took his hand and squeezed it, and they said a decade of the rosary together, Sorrowful Mysteries, for the families. He could see—when the wind again changed directions— the old tree, its back broken and bark all twisted, spikes of pale wood sticking straight up in the air. The leafy top was spread over the roof, crushing it in the middle.

She pulled him away from the window when the rain began to pelt it with a force you could feel. Then the candle went out and his mother groped for matches on the countertop. The window rattled in its frame, and the wind shrieked through the cracks in the wood. She grabbed his hand and they ran down the back steps to the first floor, and then down cellar. They huddled there together sitting on top of the steamer trunk, wrapped in an old afghan she had pulled out. It was only later that they found that the other room was six inches deep in water, and water beginning to trickle under the door to the foot of the cellar steps.

But the worst was over by eight o'clock that night when it was really dark—not a light anywhere in the sky or in the waterlogged city. The wind had died down, but it was still raining. The next morning firemen made it up their street flooded with water and rescued the poor Petersons—the McHenrys, too: they were all right after all, they had hid out in the cellar. One by one they traipsed through the backyard, each covered with a fireman's coat. There was danger, his mother said, waiting for them to file into her parlor to be warm and dry, of electrocution with all those live wires. She pointed to the tree, but it was raining too hard to see any wires; all you could see was the sodden branches wrapped around the house.

But that night, as the rain started to taper off and they thought the worst was over, a full moon was forming a huge tidal wave that peaked in the night and swept out everything on the shoreline. They heard about it from Mr. Silverman, out on the sidewalk boarding up the windows of his store, although the rain had already gotten in and soaked the shelves of dry goods and flooded the wooden floor. Jimmy had gone out with the McHenrys, and little Mavis McHenry, upon hearing the description of the terrible wave, began to cry and she didn't even have a beach house to lose, he thought, watching her red, streaky face, now buried in her mother's side. Mr. Silverman was telling the story again for the sake of some new people who had gathered around the storefront. It was an even better story: the force of the moon tide had rolled up all the water in the bay until it was a tower high and wide as the beach; it tipped its gigantic crest when it reached the sand and poured down with a tremendous crash on Warwick Neck, blew everything down, then swept it out to sea, and he *was* crying, as he pictured those broken-up houses and garages spun out in the undertow, his own house mixed in there, too.

As the days went by, he heard more stories. People had died. His mother read him an account from the special edition. A whole house, with a family still in it, was yanked from the ground and tossed into the furious river of water. But miracles occurred, too. A single survivor was saved from a collapsing beach house, floating forward on the floor like a raft, a floor so solidly built that it separated neatly from its walls after a fury of water and wind had loosened its joints, and after the foundation had caved in from the weight of the huge watery belts.

His mother took him downtown a week later to show him the damage. Downtown had been buried under three feet of water. Some of the streets were still flooded, but most of the water had spilled back into the river. People had marked the buildings with a line of paint to show how high the water rose. They went up and down the streets, but he did not ask to see the watermark on the Westminster Building, and she did not take him near that corner.

After a while, men started building a hurricane wall around the sea-edge of the city, and south along the bay. It could never happen again, the papers said, not with the wall the men built, so strong and so high. They were probably wrong, he thought; it could happen again. A storm fifty times wilder could crash those flimsy walls and sink the city in water, easy as pie.

And wall or no wall, no one ever forgot the hurricane. He dreamed about it. His favorite dream was sailing on a raft that was the floor of their house, through the streets of downtown. You could see nothing but water, deep wavy water, and a few of the tallest buildings. It was one of the most exciting dreams he ever had. He was the only person alive for miles. That's what he thought until his father came swimming up to the raft. "Dada!" he yelled as loud as he could, but his father kept swimming.

The Sacrifice

Katherine Angell lived on the second floor, Joe, her boyfriend and land-lord, on the first, and Mrs. Angell, her mother, occupied the attic rooms with their raw insulated walls. There were four gables. In three of them, the old lady arranged her possessions. The fourth contained the open stairwell that curved 180 degrees and led, through a closet, into Katherine's white living room.

Descending the stairs, Mrs. Angell made as much noise as she could, then tapped on the closet door. She did not want to surprise her youngest daughter. Katherine told her mother that there was a lock on the bedroom door, which she always kept shut, so there wasn't the least chance that her mother could make a mistake. But Mrs. Angell reminded her daughter that she was from the old school: she did not want to see that door closed, or run into Joe Renza, the landlord, parading around in bathrobe and slippers. "You don't want him to see *you* in your nightie and slippers," Katherine said to her mother. "Isn't that more like it?"

Mrs. Angell, fumbling in the coat closet to find her everyday coat and hat, tried to ignore this absurd remark. She wouldn't step foot on her stairwell unless she was fully dressed, shoes and stockings. Even in the old days, Mrs. Angell was never one to leave the bedroom before she had strapped on her foundation and rolled up her stockings. She was even more particular now. She didn't want a man to see her in pincurls, so she combed out the thin, sand-colored hair before she used their bathroom.

Katherine, one of three daughters, was the only one who had not married and who still rented. The other two had homes with their husbands and children—brand-new homes with spare rooms—but no invitation had come from Jane Ann or Martha when Mr. Angell had gone into the nursing home for good, then died. Each girl sent a monthly check for the mother's upkeep (Mrs. Angell spent the money on bingo), and there was also the pension and social security. The older girls didn't take to the idea of their old mother living in an attic, and there had been arguments for trailer parks and senior housing, but Katherine had in-

sisted on having her mother with her: being with family was more important than floor space and windows.

Katherine was forty, but had lived alone for only five years. She would
enjoy the company, she told her mother. So Mrs. Angell packed her
trunks and boxes, then had a yard sale, when the realtors sold the old
house on Fern Street. She had no girlfriends to tell, but she bragged at the
Saturday night bingo game that she was so popular, her daughter wanted
her just for the company! The girls who sat around her—Gladys, Miriam, and Eileen, all retired, all widows, all living alone—hooted with
laughter. A minute later, after I-19 was called and "Bingo!" trumpeted
through the hall, as two old men came bustling down the aisle to check
the winning numbers, Miriam piped up: "Annie," she said, "didn't you
tell us that your daughter has a live-in boyfriend?" All the girls turned
from their cards, swept free of beans and bingo markers to look at Anne
Angell, flushing red up to her sandy hair and black velvet hat, caught in a
lie. Mrs. Angell looked straight at Miriam, whose daughter had been
divorced and now had a husband who beat her: who was she to talk? The
other girls turned back to their cards; the M.C. was reaching for the first
numbered ball to start a new game. Miriam then whispered to Mrs.
Angell—loud, so the others could hear: "So why does she need *you*?
Someone is keeping her bed warm at night."

Anne Angell had a remark on the tip of her tongue, but the man called
an O-65, and she had that number on three of her twenty cards; she
reached with an unsteady hand for some beans and covered each of her
65s. For the moment, the matter was dropped.

The girls at bingo were hard, she thought later on, riding back to
Katherine's house—a pretty part of town, much nicer than where they
all had to live. (One was in a project, the other two lived by themselves in
senior housing. She knew what these places looked like—smelled like,
too.) But she got the message, not that she hadn't already figured it out:
that her daughter didn't really want her for the company, she was just
saying that. Mrs. Angell looked out the cab window—it was late, the
streets were empty, and the houses were dark. Still, the difference
between Katherine and *their* daughters, Gladys had pointed out after
they'd had their free doughnuts and coffee and were saying goodbye for
another week, was that Katherine was nice enough to lie, where theirs
told them right to their faces that they weren't welcome. "My daughter
treats me like a bum," Gladys whispered in that husky voice—smoked all
her life and wasn't about to quit now. She was grinning, but she meant it:
it had hurt. "Imagine treating your mother that way," Eileen—who had
overheard—chimed in, and now they were all talking about it again. In
the end, they agreed: Anne Angell was to be envied, even *with* the live-in

boyfriend. "Big deal," Gladys had said, "these days, everybody has one." And they all laughed. Even someone they knew, Frances Stringer—did they know her? Eileen asked, "plays bingo in Pawtucket on Saturday?"— had a live-in boyfriend. They all waited. "He's sixty," she said, patting the thin gray curls all around her hat, "and she's seventy-two!" They hooted, all except Anne, who was subtracting the difference in their ages, and trying to remember what Frances Stringer looked like. She had met her one time. The ladies poured out of the bingo hall still laughing, and stood with Peter, the young man who put each of them into a cab and sent them home, receiving a fifty-cent tip for his troubles.

She couldn't remember what Frances Stringer looked like, and who cared anyway? There had to be another reason for a boyfriend so young, she thought as she paid the cabdriver, who was also young and stretched out his hand for the money, but hadn't the courtesy to look Mrs. Angell in the eye. When she put the two dollars in his hand, he closed it and raised his index finger—what did that mean?—then drove away.

Mrs. Angell stood on the sidewalk and watched till the taxi reached the corner and the brake lights tapped on. She had never had a boyfriend. Even old Ben had never really been her boyfriend. He was a friend of the family—a printer in her father's union and a member of the Elks. He "courted" her for a couple of years—that's the word her father would have used, but all it meant was that he spent a lot of time in the house, drinking homemade wine with her father and her brother, playing cards and dominoes. He was more at home with her family than with his own and now she wondered if that was the real reason he'd married her. She turned and looked at the house—there was one light burning upstairs and Joe had left the porch light on. Maybe Katherine asked her in to hide the fact that she was living alone with a man, and Katherine was no spring chicken either.

Whenever Katherine took her mother shopping, which she did several times a week, Mrs. Angell filled the cart with things she liked: fancy jellies and premium breads, buttery breakfast cakes and creamed soups. Mrs. Angell cooked for her daughter, but preferred her own jellies and breads to the meat loaves and chicken she fixed for Katherine and Joe. Since coming to live with Katherine last December, she had had her pick of things at the grocery store and had gained weight. She was round all over, and it was only with the aid of the pink cotton foundation, its sturdy strings and straps, that she was able to squeeze into her dresses. She noted the extra thickness of her waist as she dressed one morning a few weeks later. It was a Friday, a shopping day, and she had a few minutes to spare, so she stood gazing at her nakedness in her mother's old-fashioned mirror. Her form was sandy pink in the blue light of morning. She wasn't used to seeing her body in the nude—she hadn't even looked in the days when there would have been something better to see. Then she had always dressed behind a screen, and kept a robe beside the bed in case she had to rise in the night without time to slip her nightgown over her head. The most he ever saw in thirty-five years of marriage was her broad freckled back and pale behind.

The tall wood-framed mirror tilted on its hinge and reflected some of the silver wallpaper and part of the skylight, but was too narrow to show her torso and both her arms, so she stepped back all the way to the wall, until she felt against her back, the coolness of the silver paper. Slowly she raised her eyes.

"Are you dressed, Ma?" Katherine shouted, knocking on the living-room door.

Mrs. Angell stood perfectly still: if Katherine had the notion to open that door, she would have seen everything, but she didn't. She rapped again. "Mother? Are you ready?"

Mrs. Angell looked to her bed where the pale layers of underwear were spread out over her dress, which was still on a hanger.

"Are you still up there? Will you answer?"

"I'm here," she answered, finally.

Mrs. Angell dressed and her daughter drove them to the smaller of the two grocery stores. "You stayed out late last night," said Katherine. "Win any money?"

"No," her mother said. "I didn't win a cent. Nobody won." Mrs. Angell tried to sound as disappointed as her daughter might think she felt, but she had no force to put into her words.

"You're tired," Katherine said. "I can hear it in your voice."

Katherine pulled into the parking lot, so her mother was spared the trouble of trying to remember whether she'd stayed out late or not. She did not enjoy bingo as much as before, but she didn't want to get into that right now, and not with Katherine.

When they got to the electric doors, they separated. Katherine drove a cart up and down the aisles, while her mother went and found the shelf of imported things—biscuits and cookies, soups, mustards and wine vinegars with sprigs of herbs floating in the bottles. She tried to read the labels in foreign languages, fingering the strange-shaped or -sized boxes and jars. There was always something different about these labels. The pictures of the food were too big or too detailed, sometimes just one ingredient figured on them, a grain or a few beans. She couldn't imagine buying a vinegar that had a stick in it, or a tiny jar of cornichon pickles, although Katherine said to go ahead and try it. As she wandered up one side of the imported aisle and down the other, looking at nothing in particular, Mrs. Angell felt irritated with Katherine—a good girl, but too eager to please.

There was something new on the cookie shelf, a glossy white package of French biscuits. She picked it up. This was interesting. The wrapper was plain except for the picture of the cookie. It was a square wafer— quilted brown, a braided border, layered with a wedge of chocolate carved into a schoolboy carrying a satchel of books, perfect in every detail. The boy was wearing a sailor suit. Next to him was his dog and a background of flowers and a school house. Why, she wondered, did they go to so much trouble for a cookie?

When she had raised her three, there was nothing so nice in the stores. She had bought the occasional box of Hydrox cookies or graham crackers, but mostly people made their own goodies, and bought only what they had to. Even if these handsome schoolboys had been on Abe's shelf, or Lepore's, she could not imagine bringing them home for Ben or the girls to gobble up, the girls licking the chocolate slab and leaving the cookie gnawed on the napkin, Ben breaking the square into bite-sized pieces and then dunking them in his Ovaltine.

She carried the box to Katherine's shopping cart and placed it off to one side with her purse on top of it, while Katherine was busy picking through the plastic-wrapped chicken fryers. Mrs. Angell took her daughter aside—away from the chilled counter and its white glare—to the dairy counter, even whiter and colder, but no meatman behind the glass to overhear. She told her daughter that she meant to make some of her own purchases this time and had brought money. Katherine said no, she would pay for whatever her mother wanted. But Mrs. Angell did not want Katherine to waste her hard-earned money on foolish and extravagant treats. Her daughter insisted: "I'll get it for you this time," she said, raising her voice a little.

"It's not necessary."

"It *is* necessary."

They stood there. Mrs. Angell could see that her daughter was now aggravated, so she took the box out of the cart, but Katherine plucked it out of her hand and put it back in: "Let me buy this for you, *please*," she said between her teeth.

"I wish you wouldn't."

But when Katherine wheeled her filled basket to the checkout counter and placed her order on the belt, the cookies were gone. She looked at her mother, but Mrs. Angell was leafing through an issue of *Redbook*. It wasn't until they were in the car that she said, "I thought you wanted those cookies, Ma."

"I changed my mind," replied her mother.

Katherine drove them back through the empty afternoon streets. It had not been long since her father's death, so she often took a little time off from work—vacation days and sick days—to keep her mother company. Katherine had lived at home until she was thirty-five and met Joe Renza. She had felt close to her mother—they had always done things together, shared the chores, and enjoyed a cup of tea in the afternoons when Katherine came home from work with "the scandal" about her boss (married three times, and every time the woman was older) and her coworkers. Since the father had died and Mrs. Angell had moved in, she seemed like a different woman. She was mute and watchful, and awkward with Joe, who was as nice and easygoing a man as you could find. She was too polite and always doing Katherine this or that favor, unasked, until Katherine started feeling edgy. It was like having a boarder. She didn't know her mother anymore: the woman seemed content to spend her days alone, doing the chores, watching TV, and spending the evenings up in her room with bound copies of the *Reader's Digest*. Someone had enrolled Katherine in a book club and, although the bindings were attractive, she didn't care to read the short articles. Her mother stacked the books on her own bedside table and intended, she said, to read each one. When she was finished, she was going to apply for a library card.

Katherine put away the groceries, changed her clothes, and went back to work for the afternoon. She had planned to take her mother clothes-shopping—Mrs. Angell needed a new dress—but the old lady had disappeared right after lunch, and Katherine, after tapping on the living room door, had gotten no answer.

Anne Angell was trying to sleep. She had become accustomed to long afternoon naps. She had slipped off her dress, shoes, stockings, and foundation and was lying on the bed in her slip. The sun had gone in and the attic corners filled with shadows, the only light a smoky patch visible through the skylight. The room was so dim that the numerals on the metal clock—Ben's clock—were glowing a dusty green color. She turned the clock face away so she wouldn't see the time she was wasting. On the back of the clock were the old-fashioned pins and wind-up keys. They reminded her of him (the clock was called Baby Ben!) sitting on the edge of the bed in his shorts and socks winding that clock in a burst of angry twists. He was a hasty man, tense. Everything and everyone in the house was driven along at his erratic pace, or he would turn irritable and snap at them. His bark was worse than his bite—they all knew this—but they still catered to him, to keep him calm, to keep things quiet. He had model children; it didn't take much to keep them in line, his girls, but he still exploded at the least setback or sign of imperfection: Martha with her hair uncombed and her nose in a book, Katherine dropping a toy so it clattered down the steps and made a racket. He had no interests, no hobbies: he sat in his chair, smoking like a chimney, just waiting for trouble to start. The solution—and they all knew this—was to get him to drink just enough beer before supper to relax him, but not too much. They heard the icebox door open—or not open—as they sat around the dining-room table and she helped them with homework.

She pushed the round clock farther away, tucking it behind the radio: she didn't need to know the time anymore. Looking at the face of the old cream-colored radio with its orange dial, she wondered: if he had out-lived her, would he have thought of a girlfriend? Or was he too nervous? The ladies had always liked Ben—he played up to them. A nice white shirt and a sportscoat, he could have the car washed and waxed and pick up—who? A girl like Gladys—she had sex appeal—was more his speed with her lipstick and matching polish, open-toed shoes with high heels. She wouldn't be caught dead in the old-lady shoes the rest of them wore. Ben would go for that—who wouldn't? They could go dancing, or have a few highballs, chew the fat.

She heard the outside door slam. It must be Joe, who came in every day around this time, changed his clothes (he owned a muffler shop on Broad Street), and went out again. Sometimes he met Katherine downtown for a drink after work, sometimes he just went out by himself.

She wouldn't (shaking her head for emphasis) have begrudged Ben a girlfriend. Still, it would be surprising if he had enough oomph. He never had had much. No one had expected Katherine to have a boyfriend, much less to live with one, to share—as she knew they did—a bed at night. This was harder to imagine than the girlfriend Ben might have wanted for his widower years. She reached over and pulled the clock out from behind the radio: 4:30, not that late: there was still time to lie abed and idle.

When she heard the door slam again, she looked for the face of the clock but couldn't see it. It was turned to its side and just out of reach. She felt chilled—her skin was covered with a thin sheet of moisture as if she'd been rained on. The room was completely dark except for the smoky square of skylight. She turned over on her side, wincing at the stiffness in her back and legs—she must have fallen asleep—and tried to kick the afghan, folded at the foot of the bed, onto her bare legs, but managed only to tuck her feet under it. Her mother's pretty mirror, she noticed, was a cloudy gray, although everything around it was black. Something was shimmering in the silvered glass—or was it the mirror itself shivering on its hinge?

The doorknob turned, and then she heard Katherine's slippered feet scuffling up the stairway; through the open door the lamplight streamed up the stairs and over the silver-papered walls. Mrs. Angell closed her eyes and waited for her daughter to reach the top, pad across the attic floor, and stop by the bedside. "Mother?" After a few moments, Katherine unfolded the afghan, shook it out, and let it float down and fall over her mother's back and neck. Then she turned, and said good night in a clear voice from the bottom of the steps. As the door was pulled closed, the fan of light folded up, and then was gone.

By the next Saturday's bingo, Anne Angell had gone downtown on the bus and gotten a permanent wave at Cherry's. The hair was even paler than before, more ashen than sand-colored, and the harsh curling solution had made the feathery strands brittle. Still—and everyone agreed with this—for all the damage it had done to the fine hair, it was a flattering style. Anne brushed the frizzed hair high off her forehead and the stiff cloud made her face, a narrow oval and especially the large, gray eyes, more emphatic, if a bit severe-looking. The hair had always been soft and sparse as a baby's. When she became pregnant with Jane, it had gotten even thinner and she had tried a series of stiff-curled wigs, but they didn't make wigs very nice in those days, and the gay-colored curls (honey, strawberry blonde) made her look, Ben had said, like a hoyden. So, for all those years, she had put up with the flimsy, impossible hair that always looked unkempt. She had tried perms before, but they'd always burnt the delicate strands, or they didn't take at all. Nowadays, the permanents were adapted for different hair types, the beautician—a man—had said, and they had a formula for baby-fine hair like hers. He had very skillfully parted the hair and wound it so that the entire skull was covered with intricately nested curls.

The girls at bingo had squealed with pleasure. Mrs. Angell went hatless, and they made her twirl around, patted her hair, asked over and over for the name of the shop where they'd performed this miracle, and forgot it as soon as they asked, and had to ask again.

"You look like money," Miriam said, as they sat at their usual places waiting for the man to come around with their bingo cards. "Ei," Miriam said to Eileen, who bought sixteen cards and arranged them in four rows, "doesn't she look like money?" Eileen was heaping up a pile of white beans on the right side of her cards. "The question is," she said, "is she going to *win* money?" and they all laughed.

Katherine, although surprised that her mother would do something so radical and on her own, also liked the new hairdo. She offered again to take her mother out to buy a dress to go with the hair, but Mrs. Angell didn't have the energy to go—although, Katherine noticed, she did have the energy for bingo, for gallivanting downtown and going to visit beauty shops. She had plenty of energy for her own pleasure. Katherine no longer asked her to go to the grocery store because she always said no and not to buy her anything special: she'd eat what they ate. Katherine, nonetheless, came home with a bag full of the jelly and bread and treats, and Mrs. Angell put them on the dinner and breakfast table for anyone to share. She also dug out a set of cookbooks that Katherine had stored on the living-room bookshelf for that rainy day when it might be fun to cook something elaborate.

Mrs. Angell arranged these books on the kitchen counter next to the breadbox. She read the cookbooks over breakfast and tried out recipes for Joe and Katherine at dinner. Katherine didn't have the necessary spices or staples for some of the more interesting dishes, so her mother added these items to the shopping list. At first, Katherine didn't buy any of these spices—coriander, ginger root, fresh garlic—or the staples—wheat flour, Dutch chocolate, beef soup bones, Italian rice. She bought the usual things: hamburger, chicken, chops, a few potatoes, and two or three boxed or frozen side dishes, maybe a cake mix or icebox cookies. When she came home from the shopping trip, her mother was sitting at the kitchen table writing in a pad with a book open next to it, which she closed when Katherine walked in.

"Are you planning a dinner party?" Katherine asked, as she pulled off her coat and her mother took it and hung it in the hall closet.

"*Are* you?" Katherine repeated, when the mother returned and gathered up her pad and book. "What's that you're reading?"

"A book I found," said Mrs. Angell. "I took it from your bookshelf. Don't you recognize it?"

Katherine took the book from her mother's hand. It was an illustrated book she had gotten at the supermarket, a bonus for purchasing three volumes of a tool encyclopedia for Joe: *Indoor Plants,* it was called, a collection of articles by a writer from *House Beautiful.* Katherine placed the book on top of some canned tomatoes. She told her mother she was happy she had found so many entertaining things to fill her days, but had she realized that the apartment got no direct sunlight? She corrected herself: the front windows did get a little, but most of the day the light was blocked by the house across the street. Mrs. Angell said nothing.

"Shall I put this back?" she then asked her daughter.

"Don't be silly," said Katherine in that exasperated tone she used more and more these days on her mother. "No one said you couldn't read that book. I just don't want you sending me all over town to pick up plants that are going to drop dead after a week in the dark. Do you understand what I'm saying?" she asked. "Do you?"

Mrs. Angell had to bite her tongue not to say that Katherine sounded just like her father, a killjoy. "Thanks for telling me," was all she said, but that was enough.

"Jesus Christ, Ma! Why do you always sound so persecuted? Who's persecuting you? I think you have a pretty nice life here, if you ask me. You act like I'm making you live on bread and water."

Mrs. Angell, close to the living room and her white door, turned around and looked at her daughter, whose face flamed with anger. She waited a moment, then said, "You didn't buy those things I wrote down, did you?" Before Katherine could answer, she added, "I didn't think so. That's okay, honey. Why should you?" She turned toward her door, then thought better of it. "You're treating me just fine, Kathy. You just worry too much." She opened her door and slowly ascended. "That's all."

Katherine returned to work, but that night she picked up some of the supplies her mother had listed. She forgot the coriander. While Katherine put the new groceries away, showing her mother where she was putting them, Mrs. Angell sat at the table and copied out several recipes from the main course and dessert volumes, then closed her notebook. "Where's Joe?" she asked.

"I don't know, Ma. He had to go somewhere."

"Oh."

"Why do you ask?"

"Doesn't he usually come home first—then go somewhere?"

"I don't know. Sometimes."

The mother reached over and pulled out a chair, but Katherine ignored it. She didn't feel like sitting down to an interrogation, but she didn't feel like leaving either. She scanned the kitchen to see what needed doing: squeezed the faucet cocks, refolded and draped the dishcloth over the rim of the sink, then edged into the chair her mother had pulled out for her, but jumped up again to move a magnet that had slipped down the refrigerator door.

"We don't talk like we used to," her mother said in a softened tone.

"You're not usually interested," the daughter replied.

"I wish you wouldn't say things like that."

Katherine got up to pour herself a glass of water. It was hard to get the cold-water cock to budge. She had to use both hands. "Do you want some water?"

"No," her mother said, "but I could use a little of that sweet wine."

"Joe's wine?"

"Is it his?" asked the mother. "I thought he drank beer."

Katherine found an old-fashioned wine glass of her grandmother's and poured the brown wine—muscatel—into the wide shallow bowl and up to the gold-edged lip. Her mother picked the glass up by the stem and sipped. (Was she wearing eye shadow now?) "Are you sorry you're stuck with me?" her mother asked.

Katherine glared at her. Her water glass was empty, so she got up to refill it, pried the ice-cube tray loose from its envelope of frost and cracked it against the sink, then twisted the metal dish until two ice cubes leapt out and spun into the drain. She dropped the cubes into her glass and refilled the dish with water. The cold water was cloudy. Katherine waited until it cleared. "Did I hear you right?" she said.

"I'll take a drop more, too," replied her mother, handing Katherine the empty wine glass.

"Where did I put it?" Katherine asked, scanning the counters.

"You put it away."

The mother's glass was refilled and they sat at the table again across from each other.

"How can you say a rotten thing like that? Don't you think you're being kind of childish?"

"Not if I'm right."

Katherine got up, went to the refrigerator, and opened one of Joe's Ballantine beers.

"Good idea," her mother said. "You need it."

"I don't need it!" Katherine shouted. "Don't tell me what I need! How would *you* know?"

Her mother waited. "I guess I wouldn't," she said. "At least, that's what you're telling me."

"Now you're going to the other extreme, Ma," said Katherine wearily. "That's your trouble. You act like a boarder around here. This is your home." Katherine gulped the beer, then pushed it away. Her mother pushed it back.

They drank in silence. Then Katherine piped up: "If there was anyone we should have hated, it was him. You know that. But I don't even hate him. Who has the energy for that?"

"Did you hate him, Kathy? I didn't know that."

"I didn't say that, Ma. If you want to have a conversation, you have to listen."

Mrs. Angell glanced at the clock, took a sip of wine. "It wasn't his fault he was so bad. He had awful problems," she said, ringing the glass with her fingernail. "This is too sweet, don't you think?"

"All I know is he took you for granted," Katherine replied.

"Do you think so?" her mother said, thoughtfully. "I guess maybe we didn't know anything in those days."

Katherine didn't answer.

Her mother pushed her wine glass away. "But Joe loves you, doesn't he?" she said, looking up at her daughter's reddening face, young-looking in spite of the outdated glasses and dark face powder. Was it youthful or just immature? The face blazed with color. "I didn't mean to embarrass you. Anyone can see that he does."

"Are you surprised by that?" Katherine shot back.

"Oh, I'm not surprised," the mother replied, rising to carry her glass to the sink. "I'm happy for you, Kathy. You waited a long time, and now you have what you always wanted."

Katherine considered. She waited for her mother to sit down, then took her glass to the sink and held it under the faucet. Her mother always had had a knack for saying a tactless thing. When the three sisters were grown up and began to talk to each other, they had often discussed the problem of how much pain their mother's words inflicted: how each had felt stupid, ugly, or selfish because their mother—although she never hit them, or even raised her voice—always said what she thought.

Katherine dried the beer glass, polished it, and set it on the counter. Her mother was still there. Katherine had to remind herself, before turning to face her, that her mother was old now, and deserved the extra consideration—the gourmet meals, the house plants, whatever she wanted—no matter what. But for all that, Katherine did not feel kindly or forgiving toward the person sitting behind her.

She heard her mother's chair scraping on the floor. "I like talking to my daughter," she said to Katherine's back. "You're a nice person, Kathy. And I like talking to you. Too bad you don't like talking to me."

Mrs. Angell stood and watched her daughter stalk out of the room, her neck and her back stiff with tension. When she heard the bedroom door close, she walked up to her attic. It had started raining and the sound of rain always relaxed her. The rain was falling through the open hatch in a beautiful shower of silver, not ribboned but fine and powdery, with a white smoke curling off the floor as the raindrops struck there. Now, she thought—taking off her slippers and feeling the damp planks soft under her feet—if only she could call Katherine, tell her daughter to come up to the skylight and feel this clean, cold water and how smooth it made the old boards.

But Katherine, as if she had been listening to the thought and not following any notion of her own, was there already. She had climbed the attic stairs on silent, slippered feet. She still had her stockings in her hand. She was looking at her mother standing under the open hatch in the pouring rain, an apology on the tip of her tongue, until she saw the old woman letting the rain make a puddle on the floor, probably seep down and patch the freshly painted living-room ceiling, and her voice crackled with the cruel words she had choked back from the very day when, out of the kindness of her heart, she—not the other two, whose selfish smallness they'd learned at home—invited her mother to move in.

Uncle Maggot

Darlene and Margaret, sisters, were playing in the street, "Call-ees up," when the ambulance came. They could hear it before it turned the corner blaring and screeching, and got off the street—and the ball out of the street—just in the nick of time, and were hiding behind the trellis under the porch all out of breath. When the ambulance stopped, the siren stopped too and Harold Street was quiet, except for the bluejay still squawking in the tree. They were looking where the ambulance was and saw the man jump out and unfold a stretcher. It was then that they heard commotion in the house, the screen door flew open, and that was their mother's voice.

Darlene, fourth grade, was bigger than Margaret, third grade, and told her sister just to hush up and sit quiet. She was going to sneak out around the edge of the house and get a look in the pantry window, shinnying up the side of the house and hanging from the ledge, but neither moved. They waited. In a minute they heard the door fly open again and slam against the railing of the back porch (just a stoop and concrete steps). There was a lot more commotion now. Someone turned the siren on again, and they saw (Margaret saw, Darlene had her eyes shut tight and her hands over them and was already crying) that it was him all strapped to the stretcher, his arms strapped in there, too. It was a commotion and the neighbor ladies were on the street, Mrs. Martin and Mrs. Donley and the little Donleys (little jerks they were and one tomboy), and then Margaret saw her mother climb into the back of the ambulance. She couldn't see her mother's face, but the apron was still on and shoes with no stockings. Once her mother was in, it seemed to take a long time, but finally the ambulance started moving. It turned into their driveway—Margaret could see her mother's face through the window, but then her mother turned her head. The ambulance backed out and went screaming down the street and around the corner.

Now Mrs. Martin was calling them: "Darlene, Margaret, Dar-*lee*-een!" They were holding hands and, although they were afraid of the dark dirt under the porch—anything could be down there—they hunched down together, side by side, their backs rubbing against the brick foundation, and now all red from the dust. Darlene had her legs straight out, but Margaret was just squatting, then folded her legs under her. "You're taller than me!" Darlene said, so Margaret stretched out her legs too, although she didn't like what she was feeling under them—something not exactly rocks and dirt—and would have to jump up any minute. Besides, she was crying now and ready to cry some more, and Darlene was crying, telling Margaret to get up and find out, and she said, shut up, *you* get up and find out, no *you*.

They were both crying on the hard ground, and Darlene had just given Margaret a slap, when the neighbor found them and jerked Margaret up by the arm: "You stupid little stupids! What are you *doing* under here, when your poor mother's looking all *over* for you?" And Darlene said, "You're not my mother. Leave me alone." But Margaret cried over this fresh remark, and Mrs. Martin didn't hear, but took each girl by the arm and dragged them home to face the music—red all down their play clothes, and up and down their legs, and even Darlene's hair had red dust in it.

No one was home. Where was the baby? "The baby," Mrs. Martin said, pushing a chair closer to the table and straightening a throw rug with her foot, looking all around the kitchen, walking to the window and closing it shut (although it was hot outside, not cold), "is with a neighbor." "Who?" "Oh," she glanced at the clock and walked to the sink, looked out that window and folded the dishcloth that was already folded and draped over the faucet, "with the lady downstairs, what's-her-name: Flynn. You girls have homework to do?"

Darlene looked at Margaret and Margaret looked at Darlene: didn't she know it was summertime and no one had homework in summertime?

"I don't mean homework," she said, "I mean something to keep yourselves occupied. Do you have something to do if I told you to go to your room and just sit there quiet? Could you do that?"

The phone rang and Margaret ran to get it. "No, don't you answer that, let *me* answer it." Margaret handed Mrs. Martin the receiver. "Yes, hello. This is Dotty Martin here. Who am I speaking to? No, I don't know, I'm sorry. No, she's not here. No, he's not here."

Margaret and Darlene looked at Mrs. Martin and she looked at them, but they couldn't tell from looking at her what was wrong with their father. They knew it was bad and that he might even be dead, but this wasn't the kind of thing children should get involved in: they knew that much, too.

Mrs. Martin was motioning for them to get something—what? She kept motioning while Margaret picked up first the salt shaker on the kitchen counter, then the Brillo pad, the glasses' case, and finally the cigarettes on top of the fridge. Margaret had to stand on a chair to get them, and Darlene stood there gaping. After lighting one of their father's Viceroys, Mrs. Martin leaned against the broom closet. She wasn't talking, just listening. She put a hand over the mouth of the receiver. "Why don't you girls go into your bedroom like good girls, and shut the door please? Nice and quiet now."

Margaret and Darlene looked at her a minute, then trudged into the back of the house and fought a little over *whose* room—Darlene's or selfish Margaret's, who liked to keep people and pests out. They went into Margaret's, because Darlene pushed her in and slammed the door, then they opened the door just a crack and sank down onto the floor to listen. He had had a heart attack, that's what she was saying, and it was a close call, but she thought he might pull through. He looked bad, yes, but he had looked tough for a long time. They both looked tough, a hard life with three kids and him out of work sixteen-going-on-seventeen months, the company still on strike, a shame, but—. "Excuse me!" Mrs. Martin raised her voice, and so loud Darlene blocked her ears. "Do you have that door *closed*, you little brats? (Just a minute please.)" Margaret closed the door and they both scurried to the other side of the room, squirming into the gap between the bed and the wall. But Mrs. Martin, a busybody—in her window all the livelong day, their father said, her nose into everybody's business—just came up to their door and gave it a push with her foot.

Margaret flopped onto the bed, then sat up again to look out into the street where it had all just happened. "Darlene?"

"What?"

"Nothing."

"What?"

"Did it bleed?"

"No, stupid, it bleeds on the *in*side, don't you know that much?"

"Oh."

"Look it up in the dictionary."

"There's no dictionary here."

"Look it up at school. Go to the library."

"Want to go to the libe?"

"Now?"

"Let's just go, Dar, let her find out the hard way."

Darlene took no time to think this over. They shot out the front door, and were screaming down the street before Mrs. Martin even had the wits to look for them. She was still gabbing, what their father would call a chatterbox or gasbag: she could bend an ear, they heard him say, and he said it about everybody—everybody except their mother, who didn't have

"two words to string together, nothing to say for herself, all clammed up
and pitiful." Then their mother would cry and he'd say, "Oh, look at that
one, look at the face on her, stop a clock, where's my sunshine, where's
my baby sweetheart?" Their mother would cry louder and sometimes
Margaret, a baby, would get scared and cry too, but usually she just hid
in the den behind the couch and waited for it to be over.

When they got to Academy Avenue, two lanes of traffic and cars
parked on both sides, they crossed and stood in front of the cigar store,
waiting to cross the other way. Margaret looked down the street toward
downtown: "Hey."

"What?"

"Instead, why don't we go to the hospital?"

They discussed this, considered the possible punishments and dismissed
them. "Where's the hospital?"

"Which hospital?"

"I don't know. You're the one who's so smart."

They walked the length of Chalkstone, a long ways, and came to Roger
Williams Hospital. It was on their side of the street, and along the way
they had passed Mrs. Cane's (sewing), Mrs. Nolan's (candy and funny
books), the 5&10 (knitting needles and nail polish), the Castle Theater
(movies and cartoons), the Spa (hot chocolate), the TV and Radio store
(picture tubes), and other places, including Del's Lemonade, the Esso
station, and Diorio's Lounge (Italian food and highballs). The hospital
was in its own block—no houses or stores around it, just a big parking
lot. It was hot and sunny and Darlene and Margaret rested on the curbstone. Darlene had tar on her shoe and Margaret was scraping it off with
a stick.

They didn't know how long they'd been sitting—long enough to scrape
off most of the tar, to take the sneaker off, empty the stone out of it, put it
back on, lace it, test the tar by tapping it—when Darlene spotted their
mother driving by in a taxicab, and screamed. At first, no one heard, then
they saw the cab skid to a stop in front of the Esso station, and went
running down the street as fast as they could (Margaret had to go back to
pick up her library card, all folded up in a soft roll on the curbstone—no,
in the gutter).

By the time Margaret ran back to the cab, Darlene was already crying,
but their mother wasn't. Margaret felt herself about to cry. The seat of
the taxi was hot and her mother put out her hand to Margaret. Margaret
took it; it was hot, and when her mother squeezed, her diamond ring
stuck into the side of Margaret's finger. Then she let go to say something
to Darlene, to give her a hankie and tell her to blow her nose. Margaret
wanted to cry, but couldn't. Darlene was asking about Daddy, but talking

in such a low voice that Margaret couldn't hear the question. That's when they both heard. They listened and their mother told them the whole story, and then told them the story again.

Later that day, after supper, when Margaret—or Maggot, as Patsy McManus called her, and Margaret sometimes liked it, sometimes didn't—was swinging on the back-stoop railing, her belly button showing, and Patsy trying to poke it with a stick, Margaret told Patsy the story. "See, he's got a bad heart, always did." (Patsy was hitting the railing with her stick.) "My mother says he's on the danger list."

"No he is not. You're lying."

"Yes he is so."

"He's off it."

"No he is not." Margaret jumped from the stoop to the ground and ran around the house, stopping in the backyard. There was a slab of stone, an old curbstone, and she sat on it and started to dig up pinching bugs so she could show Patsy. There was one—she picked it up carefully and put it on the stone, but it ran right off. Patsy sat down. "Is your father going to die?" Margaret didn't know. "Are you going to cry?" Margaret told Patsy to mind her own beeswax. "My mother told me today to say a little prayer," said Patsy, "and I did. I said a 'Hail Mary' and a 'Glory Be.'"

Margaret looked up to see if Patsy was lying. "My father's almost dead."

Patsy jumped off the stone and jumped back on it. "No he isn't. You're lying."

"Yes he is so, my mother told me."

"I'm going to tell on you."

"Go ahead, see if I care."

Patsy sat on the stone. "Are you going to cry?" Margaret put a pinching bug in Patsy's hand and Patsy gave it back to her. Patsy then sat next to Maggot, her friend, and they were silent a minute, until Patsy took her fist and pounded out a song ("My mother and your mother were hanging out the clothes") on Margaret's sweaty knee. ("My mother gave your mother a punch in the nose.") Margaret screamed and Patsy tried to scream over her scream: "WHAT COLOR WAS THE BLOOD?"

Darlene was playing by herself: house. Her husband was late for work and a pie in the oven, a lot of commotion with the babies and the squawking ducks. Where were the ducks? The ducks, she told her husband, Al Moody, were in the bathtub. He said it: bat tub. They're in the bat tub. The children were underfoot and Darlene was standing in the doorway crossing her legs and sticking her lips out for Al Moody to give them a kiss. "Give us a kiss, right here," said Darlene, striking the lips with her finger. "Here, give us one." But Al was figuring out a way to get around her, or go out the front door. This made Darlene start to swear, and throw a shoe, a barefoot sandal, red, across the room and against the bureau.

"What are you doing in there?" asked her mother. Darlene had heard her mother walk down the hallway. "Nothing."

Her mother entered the bedroom—still carrying the dishtowel—and sat down on the bed. "Who were you talking to?"

"I wasn't talking."

"I could hear you, you were talking a blue streak in here." Her mother got up to go back.

"Ma?"

"What?" Her mother walked up to the little square mirror over Darlene's bureau and looked at herself.

"Ma?"

"What?"

"When I grow up—."

Her mother was holding up strands of front hair to check for gray ones; Darlene had seen her do this before. "Yes? What are you looking at?"

"Nothing."

"Finish what you're saying and let me get my work done."

"I'm going to marry"—she thought a minute—"Father McElroy."

"He's a priest, you can't marry a priest." Her mother looked into the mirror again. "Are you being fresh just to start up some trouble?"

"I know someone whose name is Al B. Moody. I'm going to marry him."

"Who's Al B. Moody?"

"Al B. Moody."

"Yeah, I heard you: who is he? One of your little friends' fathers?"

"You said it. No, he's a movie star."

Her mother turned around, still holding a strand where there were some gray ones, but she had already pulled one and—not paying attention to what she was doing—it *wasn't* gray. "Are you going to start lying again?"

"When's Daddy coming home?"

"Answer me!"

In bathrobes and slippers, Darlene and Margaret were overhearing their mother talking to Mrs. Flynn on the back stairs, and burping the baby. Darlene was pushing Margaret with her hard hip, and Margaret was being crushed into the doorpost, until ("*Stop* it, you!") she dug her five fingers into Darlene's arm—and then put a hand over Darlene's ratty mouth so she couldn't scream back. They were both out of breath and almost lost their balance, when they heard the kitchen door close. Darlene put a finger on her lips, and pushed her face, her eyes all popped, right into Margaret's. Margaret pushed the ugly face away, but they were both quiet a second so they could listen.

But there was nothing to hear, nothing had happened, nothing but nothing. Then the phone rang, and someone came in the door, answered it, and they heard the same conversation all over again. He wasn't good, that's what they heard, but he wasn't suffering, he was peaceful and his heart had stopped in the night, but it had started up again. Margaret could picture it: the heart thinned into blood and spilled into a flat puddle until they put something under him like you put under a flat tire and pumped it up. She was showing Darlene how—all crouched on the floor pumping with her hands. Then, she said, it's like a heart again, all pushed together into a bump and back in the stomach. They had to stick all the needles back into him and take his temperature, give him an enema and pat his eyebrows with witchhazel to cool them off.

When they heard their mother—and now the baby was crying—they leapt onto Margaret's Hollywood bed. "What's your bed called?" the kids were always after Margaret to say. "What's a Hollywood bed?" "Use your head," Margaret would say, because she didn't know either, and didn't think stupid Darlene knew, or she'd ask her.

"Are you asleep?" they heard over the loud baby's crying. Their mother pushed the door open, then went out again. She came back, without the baby, and now the baby was quiet. It had something to suck on, or had a finger in its mouth.

Their mother sat on the bed and the two girls leaned their backs against the smooth plastic headboard. Margaret loved this headboard, all gray and marbly; sometimes she kissed it and ran her hand along the smooth border. It was filled with air, you could feel the air right through the skin of it. Margaret made a little hole for her head and put her head in it. Darlene had given her a kick under the covers, but Margaret ignored it, planning tomorrow morning to make a hand like a spider and crawl the spider on Darlene's sleeping feet, and strangle them!

Their mother was sitting there with her foot, in a nylon stocking and a flat, going up and down, up and down. "Are you settled?" she asked. She was fixing the bedspread over them, which they liked. Their mother had a hand on Margaret's side and on Darlene's side, smoothing their covers.

They were hearing about their Daddy (Al B. Moody, they thought, even since Darlene had told the story and told it again. No it is not. James Albert O'Connell, James Al O'Connell, or Mr. O'Connell, as the brats next door called him. JAO, the people at work called him—at first, Margaret thought it was Jail. Daddy is what *they* called him, but they didn't like to hear *her* call him that because he wasn't exactly her daddy.

Your dad, she called him sometimes. That was better and it didn't make Margaret's belly ache).

Their mother's eyes were teary, but she was still talking, and Darlene and Margaret listening so hard, they didn't have time to think about crying. They were going to be big girls, she was telling them, she was sure they were, and a help to their mother and their baby sister. And they were trying to catch up with the rest of the things she was saying, and figuring out *when* they were going to have to be big girls, and how come.

One thing was the usual thing: "I know," she said, "how you love your Daddy," and that got Margaret thinking: honor thy father and thy mother, thou shalt not kill, thou shalt not commit adultery. She was trying to picture her father, but all she could picture was Grade 2, Mother Mary John, Room 1, when the principal came in and pss-pss-pss to Mother Mary John, and then: "Miss O'Connell, please leave your place and come up here, Miss." Margaret F. O'Connell followed the principal, Mother Agates, out of Room 1 and into the corridor, and up the stairs, past grade 6, grade 7 and grade 8, and into the principal's office, standing by the desk when the principal sat down. That was his first heart attack, but Margaret (Darlene came in right after, with Mother Perpetua holding her hand, holding Margaret's hand, too, and staying with them—she was nice, everyone liked her) thought she said hot attack. Now she knew better, but then Darlene had corrected her. "*Hard,* hard attack!" but Darlene was wrong. She had pictured it, all heated up and hard as a rock, dead as a doornail, heart and soul, blowing hot and cold, bluebird bluebird in and out my window, die and go to heaven, wake up and ring the fire alarm—who touched that fire alarm?— and right to the bad boys' school, I mean the bad girls' school, up to the home for the orphans, St. Vincent the Poor. "No!" Darlene had said, "St. Vincent the *Paw!*" Their mother said they were both wrong, wash your mouth out, croak and fall down the toilet.

Now she was finished. Was she finished yet? Margaret had heard what she said and was still hearing it, but she was also thinking. Was she thinking, or not paying attention? She heard, she told her mother. "Are you listening to me, my girl?" Y-E-S spells yes, and you shall not be IT. Anybody round my goo shall be IT! Y spells y-o-u.

"Say goodbye to Daddy." "Bye, Daddy." "Wave bye to him." "Was that him?" "That's his window." Bye Daddy, Daddy-o, Kookie, Kookie, lend me your comb. "He can see you, but you can't see him." "Can he see me?" "He's with God and the angels, but he's there behind that window, see?"

In navy-blue spring coats, maryjanes, and white anklets, light summer hats with First Communion dresses, Darlene and Margaret saw him flat out in the casket (which rhymes with basket). Patsy had said, "Watch out his hand doesn't fly out of there and slap your bottom." Darlene told Patsy Mac to shut up your face, and Patsy Mac—all dressed up with taps on her shoes, white with a white buckle (they had lined up their feet so they could see the shoes all in a row)—said it again.

Margaret knelt in front of her father's casket basket, but his hand, with the ring whose red stone she liked so much, stayed down there, deep inside and surrounded by the pure white cloth with no wrinkles, folded all even and smooth, and all puffed out, filled with soft air, tisket a tasket, green and yellow casket.

In her ear, her mother was telling her, and in a crying voice, "Say goodbye to Daddy now," but Margaret didn't want to. She didn't want to talk out loud, and that's what her mother wanted: say it out loud so everyone can hear. N-O spells no. She had heard Darlene, sickening sweet, say goodbye in a little tiny babyish voice and everyone was crying and choking, except Margaret. She could see him, his eyes were closed and his hands had a rosary in them, black beads like the nuns had, but he wasn't praying, he was lying, and if you said boo, he wasn't going to lift a finger to talk back or do anything, so why say it? Someone was next to her on the kneeler; it was her uncle, Uncle Dick dickie bird sitting in a tree, k-i-s-s-i-n-g, and he talked; she couldn't believe he was talking out loud.

"Jimmy" (Uncle Dick O'Connell was their father's baby brother, "little brother," they still called him), "Margaret and I," Uncle Dick held her hand up in the air for Jimmy to see, way down in there—. But Uncle Dick couldn't get another word out to save his life; he was all filled up, so Margaret, big mouth, *all* mouth, piped up:

"Jimmy!" she said, because he had said it—a big voice, a big girl, a shrill voice, very penetrating, as they were always telling her: "This is Maggot." (Afterwards they told her all about it and she laughed, but her mother wasn't laughing then.)

"And Uncle Dick, Dick and Uncle Maggot, Ma, Darlene and all the relatives. We're here and here we are and we're here, all here to see you and say goodbye, so long ladies, farewell gentlemen, good night sweetheart, see you in the morning."

She stopped talking. It was quiet. She started singing: "We were sailing along, on Moonlight Bay. You could hear the voices singing, they seemed to say—." Now she was crying and choking like everyone else, but she didn't get the beating she deserved, and that she thought she might get right then and there—and Darlene thought so, too—but she didn't.

They reminded her of this all that year and all the next year. Then people forgot it—that she had sung and done a song and dance at her father's funeral wake. People forgot it. They remembered it later on, when she had forgotten it, or thought she'd forgotten it. Uncle Dick said, his arm around her, "People were so mad at you, such a little imp. But then they liked it. They liked it so much"—and here Uncle Dick gave her neck a hard little squeeze—"they *all* talked to him. They all got up and talked to him, and we all sang back at the house until everyone was all cried out. Then we buried him."

And then? someone said. People were enjoying this conversation from so many years ago, and they were all picking at their food and settling in for the story, just the kind that Uncle could tell so well, and that Margaret could tell. But Margaret, not usually so quiet, was quiet. Darlene was saying how clearly she remembered when they came for him that day: "We hid—you don't remember this, Margaret, but I do—under the porch. I was scared, you weren't." Darlene was looking at her: "Are you listening?"

Mr. and Mrs. Bull

There were twenty cows on the little hill, brown on white, or white on brown, and one bull, all golden and jittery. They were numbered—each had an orange tag driven through its left ear. The bull was standing on his own grassless space, tapping a foot on the hard ground, kicking up a plume of dust. "What's *his* name?" I asked my uncle, who was standing behind me with the camera. "Mr. Bull," he said. "Don't get any closer."

"Mr. and Mrs. Bull," I said, as he snapped the picture.

In his one-piece farm suit with the heavy zipper from leg to throat, his ski hat, orange boots and orange gloves, my uncle didn't look seventy years old, but he had never looked sixty years old, or even fifty. He always looked about forty or forty-five—even when he was thirty and I was just three, in that one picture, with my arm around his knee and my head just under his whiskey glass. You could never see his eyes in a photo. Like glass eggs, his lenses gave back only glass when the light dazzled their surface. But if you got up close, the eyes were there, startled-looking, pale blue against freckled skin.

He snapped my picture in the two-degree cold, posing me against the frozen beef, and then I ran to the truck where Aunt Evelyn was plumped on her seat, rosy and overheated, already talking by the time I closed the door. My eyes were still on him in his farmyard, closing the gate so the cold cows wouldn't slip away and off to New York—along with the glossy Mr. Bull, his slick back as red as my uncle's hair once was, but now all white, and bristling like a rooster's comb as he skinned off his ski cap, and turned his face away from the commands and addresses spilling from my aunt's mouth. "Quiet down, Evie," he said. "It's only 8:30 in the morning."

Heading home, with the wire-haired dog jumping at the grill and fenders, the truck lurched over the bumps of the dirt road, rigid from weeks of unseasonable cold. Later that day, Christmas day, my uncle would go out again with an ax to cut holes in the cow ponds and in the water trough, frozen and refrozen until a dense and cloudy white. I listened to the tongues of "41" and "22" rasping across the dry surface.

With a shovel I gathered the chunks of ice and flung them out of the pond. A cow was edging closer to the hole I was clearing. I moved, and it lowered its huge head until the nose was submerged and the thick tongue splashed up water; then there were two, three heads jammed in the small circle, and more coming. My uncle was making fresh cuts in the pond and I followed with my shovel—the cows alert and watching—until the pond was broken in half a dozen places, but steadily closing over again: now the first hole was sealed with a fine layer of ice and soon opaque with thickening slabs.

It hadn't been that cold a winter, they told me. It was a mild winter with hardly any snow, but then it was a cold Christmas, a cold December. My cousin Sheila, as thin as my uncle and red-haired, was watching her pale children tear wrapping paper from the flimsy cardboard boxes that held the new sweaters and doll sweaters, pink plastic doll cups and rigid doll houses. The floor was a maze of colored paper and ribbon, and Sheila, stepping over little hands and legs, placed her thin feet amidst the clutter, and bent from the waist to photograph the children. I was sitting on the hearthstone, warming my back, Uncle Jack next to me. He was wearing the new tweed jacket just opened and a tight fit over his flannel shirt and sweater. "Handsome—he's still a handsome man," my aunt said and my uncle grinned, all teeth and invisible eyes. She had gotten a ten-button blender and electric broom. These and the scarves and pastel towels she had opened—gifts from the sisters in Maine and in Massachusetts—were already stacked in a neat pile against the wall, at a little distance from the toys and paper balls, the small, tense faces and busy fingers.

Uncle Jack put out his large hand, so I transferred the glass of champagne to my right hand, then onto the scratchy hearth to hold his hand with both of mine, so cold as they always were. He rubbed my hands and blew on them, until the children and Sheila turned to look. Both children, Gay and Sara, were already on their bare feet, struggling across the cluttered floor, to collapse over their granddad's knees. Sheila sat on my other side and we were all quiet for a minute, even the children. My aunt looked up from where she sat, writing Sara's name on the "birth" certificate that had come with the new doll.

I hadn't been to see them in ten years. I hadn't been there when Edward and Sheila bought their prize-winning house (in its architecture and use of the site, the Sunday magazine had said, the most interesting house in all of southern Missouri), and hadn't been there when Edward left the house, and my aunt and uncle sold their cottage on an acre of land, with a couple of cows and some straggly trees, to move in. The "big house," my uncle wrote, and he always referred to it this way, is too much for one woman, although later he would say not big enough for two, battling over the pots and pans, the bedtime cookies and milk. Actually, he wrote, it's your aunt who takes care of the children, and I take care of the "critters." What he liked about this part of the world, he said, was that there were more critters than people. It was working out, everybody was happy, but they were glad to see me, he said; they had missed "Cousin Alice." Now, you see, everybody's here, he said, and for Christmas.

They—Sheila and Aunt Evelyn—were still awkward around me, and I'd been back a week—longer than I'd ever imagined staying—but he wasn't. We fell into our old ways as soon as the taxi dropped me at Box A, Old Spring Road, and my uncle got to talking to the driver, the only taxi in the four tiny rural towns, and a customer of the only laundromat, owned by my uncle, who would spend his afternoons there, once the cows had been watered and fed, the fences repaired, the gardens weeded and irrigated, and any errands to town—for groceries and gadgets, paper-back novels and videotaped cartoons—run; when children, mother, and daughter were settled in the house for a quiet afternoon by the pool, or in the playroom. He invited the driver in and we all had a drink and relaxed, "Unk" sitting next to me on the couch and rubbing my neck, giving me the pleasure of hearing again, after so many years, that raggedy laugh and the whiskey smell that came with it.

"Look up, Al, I want to take your picture with Dad and Mom," Sheila was saying, holding her small camera. The children arranged themselves around us in their soft pajamas, each with a toy, and Aunt Ev still holding the doll birth-certificate, pressing the paper against *Black Beauty,* present from Auntie Alice.

"Take one"—Sheila handed Uncle the camera—"of me and Cousin Alice. Who knows when I'll see her again?"

"Do you want me in this one?" my aunt asked Sheila, and the two girls chimed in.

"No, just me and Al." Sheila took my hand and sat closer, but Aunt Ev and the girls moved closer too, Sara dropping across our laps, knocking the pencil and paper out of Gram's hands, and had to be told Santa would be cross, and might take everything back if she acted like a such a naughty girl. This made Gay cry, but Sheila was already up to put an album on the stereo, a new album: soft rock versions of carols and holiday songs. "This is the best one in years," she said, as Gram took Gay on her lap and whispered that she had talked to Santa and he'd promised that he wouldn't snatch any of Gay's toys because Gay was a good girl, whereas Sara—. And now Sara was crying.

"Stop the blubbering," Uncle Jack said.

Sheila said that breakfast was almost ready, and then, over her shoulder to me, "I bet you never listen to music like this!"

Ten years ago Uncle Jack was still in California, trying to get used to it after the first five lonely years in the strange climate—an orange or grapefruit grove (as he would say) on every street corner, then orchard after orchard lopped away to build groves of ranch houses and garden apartments. "They call them that," he said, "but the garden is just a memory. They don't build the apartment till they plow up the garden." The one and only job he ever had as a boss was out there. The plant in Gloucester had sent him out when business was good and there was enough capital to open up a West Coast branch, with Unk—who'd started out a foreman on the floor—as manager and "veepee," as he called it. But the economy faltered, the industry all but died, and in a recession year following the oil crisis, what was left of the shop was auctioned off. It wasn't Unk's fault: everyone told me this but him. He never said whose fault it was. He got busy that year, and through the years following, running a couple of laundromats near San Bernardino, in one of those frantic, sun-broiled towns built on the ranches, farms, and orchards there before. It was an easy and stable business, and in those years he learned how to repair the machines and talk to the customers, to protect his stores at night from thieves and vandals, and from the packs of teenagers with a liking for the Coke machines and the bright, empty rooms. He had also taught himself how to paint and draw pictures and how to fly small planes, and when his interest in planes and landscapes faded, he walked to the town library every day and read the fiction, starting with A for Anonymous, he said.

What he had to work to forget (I knew this, and so did Sheila and Aunt Ev, although they'd never admit it) was not mistakes or the business failure—it was home, Gloucester, where he'd been born: it was the ocean, the winter, the maple trees and saltbox cottages, and, most of all, his boat. He'd had two boats, the latest and best a fishing boat he had traveled up to Nova Scotia to buy—a beat-up wood hull, which he spent a month sanding, patching, and painting, overhauling the engine—and then sailed it down as soon as it was warm enough to launch. I remember the day he came back: he called us from Maine somewhere, where he had timed his return to the hour. We waited in Rockway Cove with a picnic lunch of clams and lobster, potato salad, peaches, tomatoes, and blueberry pie, a bottle of pink champagne and one of whiskey. Even my aunt was thrilled as he came sailing down the cove; we could see the gray boat, so different from the others, and sunk so low in the water (a little too low, we found out later) and completely bare of any nautical adornment.

Then finally we could see him, his glasses blazing in the sunlight, when he threw Sheila the rope and she pulled the smooth, wide boat up to the dock and we all hopped on, kisses and hugs, and the sharp smell he had of dampness and salt, three nights and three days out on the boat. What was harder to put behind him—or behind any of us—was this.

But he did put it behind him. In the years he was reading novels and stories, he built a model of the Novi boat—the last boat, sold in Ipswich in 1965—and the little boats he'd had before. He moored this "mobile boatyard," as he called it, on his chest of drawers, then shoved off and developed an interest, as Aunt Ev put it, in racing up and down the foothills on a motorbike, often taking Sheila with him. They had in common not only the restlessness, but the strong, athletic bodies, almost fleshless, and the pale skin, quick to burn. She flew and sailed, biked and ran, waterskiied and even followed him into the deep sea with mask and tanks. Her main love, like his, was the ocean, the gray-green Atlantic north of Gloucester, whose waters, frigid and seaweedy, were, even in summertime, hooded in fog.

Sheila's in-laws, closer to our family than to their own son (who had moved farther west and now owned a motel and restaurant in Phoenix) came for breakfast and brought with them—the mother and two married daughters—several egg casseroles. Uncle Jack grilled many pounds of sausage and bacon, and my aunt had spent all the waking hours of the 24th baking breads, rolls, muffins, pies, cookies, and cakes, something she'd always done and loved to do, but as she got older (Sheila had been telling me) her cooking skill had gotten even better: her sweets were more delectable, perfect in form, and she was never satisfied with enough for one family, but baked goodies sufficient for all our families, whose ranks had thinned out, separated by time and distance—the families of her sisters, still in New England, and the little families of the nieces and nephews, our grandmother's family in New York and the in-laws in Chicago, her first husband's family in Connecticut, now many of them dead, or living in even greater isolation one from the other. Sheila didn't have to say this: Aunt Ev's concentration while mixing, buttering, and measuring, while sticking the gingerbreads and banana breads, the angel cakes and blueberry muffins (as her own mother had done) with a hatpin; and the even quieter intensity of frosting and decorating, of unmolding and cooling, covering with papers and in boxes and wiping all the kitchen surfaces, after washing a mountain of pans and bowls, spoons and strainers—all these deft and efficient motions suggested to me, sitting near her and running the occasional, idle errand, all the different kitchens, the ones I knew and the ones I didn't—and all the faces in them, Christmas and Easter, Thanksgiving and the Fourth of July.

Our breakfast table, a huge teak slab that filled Sheila's Wedgwood-blue dining room—then flooded with midmorning sun, with no mists or smoke to mute its blinding glare—was heavy with dishes and crammed with people, but strangely somber and quiet. The six children seated around their respective parents were sleepy from a restless night and predawn rising, and the adults from a short night and a morning spent drinking coffee and then champagne, or champagne, then coffee with a Bloody Mary. The conversation, when not about the last-minute buying and assembling of complicated electronic toys, was about holiday parties, new and different hors d'oeuvres recipes, weight gained and lost, and the ways in which each house was changing in color, shape, rugs, or furniture; and, eventually, how missing relatives were all the same and fine; how old each of those present seemed to feel with so many Christmases already past and barely remembered, and with children of advancing ages and *their* Christmas histories—but young, too, as the old ways still prevailed, and important things hadn't changed so very much, and never would.

You're wrong, my uncle was saying, things *had* changed.

"Oh, always the killjoy," my aunt replied. "You know what Phil means."

But Uncle Jack went on. "Everything is different now. Ask *her*," he said. "She's not down here in the boonies. She's out in the world, and nothing is the same. Right, Al?"

I hadn't been paying close attention to a familiar conversation. I smiled, but I could feel all the eyes on my face, waiting for the answer, and already not liking it.

"Never mind now," my aunt said, removing an empty vegetable dish and replacing it with yet another fragrant pie. We sipped more coffee, laced with brandy and Irish whiskey, and tasted cuts of the Christmas pies and cakes. Two of the youngest children had fallen asleep and were carried upstairs by a father, followed by a mother, who stayed up there and fell asleep herself. The table was being cleared by my aunt and Sheila's sister-in-law; Sheila gathered paper and ribbons from the second unwrapping, and stuffed them in a plastic bag.

One of the husbands, a Springfield businessman, moved from his end of the table to mine and Uncle Jack's, and asked me what it was exactly that I did. Was I in business? Before I could answer, he said that I didn't look much like Sheila's side of the family, and that he would never have recognized me—that I didn't look much like the picture from Sheila's wedding, either. And, he went on—and Uncle Jack grinned—I didn't have a Boston accent like they all did; I didn't have any accent he could recognize: Who did I talk like?

My aunt had drifted over to the table. "She doesn't talk like any of us."

"My old Alice—" my uncle said, but he was interrupted by my cousin's children, who were fighting over the new dolls, lined up by Sara with the old dolls—the same type of doll with (the package and ads insisted) a slightly different face on each. Sara wanted Gay's doll to sit with the old dolls, five of them exactly alike and all dressed up for the holidays. But Gay wanted her doll, with certificate and clothes, to be with her own things, for Gay—like her grandmother—was neat and possessive, and had stacked her presents far away from Sara's. The doll—"Alison" they called it—was returned to Gay, and Sara told one more time not to bully her little sister and to enjoy the toys in her *own* pile. The rest of the table was cleared and the Springfield businessman went up to take a nap with his wife. Uncle Jack lay on the couch and the children played their pink tape recorder, sitting under the tree, while Sheila, my aunt, and I loaded the dishwasher and scrubbed the pots. "You never told him what you do," my aunt said. "He asked you specifically, but you never answered."

I said I wasn't ashamed of what I did, and Aunt Evelyn replied, "No one thought you were. That's not what I meant. I only meant that you should have answered. You never say anything and we all like to hear you talk, don't we, Sheila?"

"We *like* to hear you talk, my old Alice," Sheila said with a smirk.

"Well, don't make fun of it," Aunt Evelyn said, turning back to the sink where there was just a soapy scum. All the dishes were washed and dried, all the pies and cakes were covered, and all the hot food boxed and refrigerated. The house was silent. "Well," my aunt said, "I don't see why I can't take a nap, if everyone else is."

I put on my coat, although I knew it wasn't enough, and a hat and scarf I found in the closet, and walked up the hill over the first pasture where some of the cows had gathered around the coil of hay, nibbling with drawn-back lips, while others sat folded up on the hard ground. When they heard me, two struggled on frozen legs to rise and totter over, but once they saw I wasn't holding anything for them, they settled back on the ground again, looking at me with their wide faces. The pond was solid, as it had been earlier, but the trough water was protected under a plate of floating ice.

The day I left, both pond and trough were slushy; just one night had brought the temperature up 30 degrees. Uncle Jack got up at five and woke me shortly after for the long trip to Springfield and a seven o'clock flight. We drove the hour before the sun rose, when, all quiet and dark, the houses and trees seemed penetrated by night. Although it was not pitch black, the sky seemed even darker. My uncle and I talked a little at the airport. We inspected each other and he said, "You haven't changed, Alice. You look exactly the same." I told him he hadn't either, but he had: his hair was all white and his features were sharper and separated out, as if the flesh was receding, leaving just the eyes and cheekbones.

He had been quiet in the warm truck. We drove past fields and farmhouses, where the only sign of life was the little windmills churning the water in the ponds—so they wouldn't freeze, he explained. "We're going to get one," he said. "They cost, but it's worth it." The car wheels were singing on the blacktop at a slightly higher pitch than the drone of the heater and air whining through the cracks in the windows.

I was thinking, long before we detected the gold line in the rearview mirror and the slight development in the view, as the scene from the highway became even less solid, that my own life, as these ten years came to an end on Christmas 1984, was emerging from a sort of planetary night to something softer, and that I would begin, like these trees and houses, to blend into the surrounding air, as objects and the space around them fused in the incremental dawn. The full light, when the elements separated again, was in the distance, and maybe never attainable—not at least to someone like me, taking so long.

He, I was thinking, had taken time and was still taking it, letting it force him out and change him. He had not wasted time; he let it eat into his sides, grind into him. I remembered when my Uncle Cam, the husband of my mother's third sister, was dying, having worked his way up to the top of a small company, only to be forced out when it was taken over by a national chain and three younger men from out-of-state were made vice-president in a department Uncle Cam alone had run. That year, Uncle Cam, beset by thirty years of unacknowledged illnesses, and just as many years of drinking and gourmandizing, received all his diseases at once, and had already come close to death several times when, exhausted, he died in a moment when everybody thought that he was pulling through. My uncle spent this same year sending his brother-in-law long, handwritten letters touching on matters present and past—recalling the years when they lived in adjacent states and bought their first boats, Cam's "plastic" and outfitted with the latest nautical gizmos and comforts, Jack's small, leaky, and barebones. The letters came often, and Uncle Cam, according to my mother, was flattered—even touched, but my uncle wasn't being kind. He was familiarizing himself, I think, with the path that lay ahead in that growthless part of life called age, with the ruts and gulleys that death carves into an overworked field. He was anticipating—and in that way, more than in any other, I was like him.

The sun's bright face, with its orange and sapphire rings, slipped into the first degree of its arc, and the vague surrounding shapes now hardened into farmhouses, scrubby trees, and the little earth-knobs called the Ozarks—and we were still driving. I knew there wouldn't be many more times like this. Uncle Jack had been my first family friend, the one who had tolerated my lazy, sleepwalking ways, but who could still savor a sharp remark. He and Aunt Ev had taken me in that summer when battles at home had reached a pitch where explosions, cuffs, screams, and over-turned chairs were a daily occurrence. I was 18, ready to go off to college. I spent that peaceful summer riding back and forth to the airplane fac-tory where Uncle Jack had gotten me a job on the switchboard. We took our bag lunches out to the docks and bays, to brackish salt ponds and dusty inlets. When the family went up to Maine, we stayed behind, making a supper from cans, drinking whiskey and Coke, going night-fishing and watching the stars.

But for all the time we spent together, there wasn't a lot of talk. I was shy, leery of boring him with an eighteen-year-old's chat. (At the time I was in love with a machinist and was often included in the slumber parties of older girls, who were willing to share their boy troubles with an eager listener.) How could any of this—the people and things I mooned over day and night—entertain a 45–year-old uncle? I had a total of one date with the machinist, who took me to a stock-car race and then straight home after. There was something, he must have figured, that a girl like me couldn't give him. I remember, in my shock at being so rudely dropped, telling my uncle that no one, I was sure, would ever want to marry me. What he said then (*"I* could, Alice"—or something like that), as we stood in the kitchen—I was washing, he was wiping—I'll never forget.

But, at the time, I just felt stunned. My aunt's bright kitchen, with its then-cold oven and rotting fruit in the big blue bowl, was still suffused with smells of roasts, cakes, and muffins. It was an awkward moment, lasting no more than the time it took to say the words and for their echo to die out in my ears. Next morning, things were back to normal. Walk-ing to the car, I received the usual rebuke about deficiencies in my appearance—a run in my stockings, wrinkles, shoes that needed repair. Then we drove the ten miles to work in our usual silence.

As we neared the airport that December dawn, the highway lights were still on, making the new, warming day seem old already. I was tired, but Unk—a full day of farm chores ahead of him—was wide awake. I got the bone-crushing hug, and a second, more thoughtful one, then I was whisked, along with the other drowsy passengers, out to the tarmac, up the flight of steps, and into the sleek body of the jet.

2

Odds

The day she got married, the ground was covered with a hard crust of snow, everyone was still alive, and the wedding itself, with the reception that followed, was the very last of our family reunions. My sister was getting married for the second time and to a man she hardly knew. That was a custom in our family: to date a lot of men who could have been our brothers, or who attended the same parochial school and had worn the same cheap blue uniform, then marry the one who came along with a foreign-sounding name, and whose every word and gesture was a mystery—at least to us, who'd grown up in a neighborhood where everyone knew everybody, and nothing ever puzzled us. Diane was marrying a man named Luciano, with a bulldog face and dark, shiny eyes. My mother thought he looked insane—but with a second marriage, I reminded her, you ask fewer questions of your children. My sister had been lonely; she hated living alone, she hated blind dates, and didn't want to become a fixture in the circle of girls buying strips of theater tickets and signing up for tap-dancing at the Y. After a couple of years alone, she joined a dating service and went out with a chef from Newport, a Barrington insurance man, and a psychiatrist with grown children. Then she met Luciano, a plumber, and they broke away from the planned dates and stopped paying dues. That much my mother had told me.

When I came home for a visit, Diane added a few details to the picture. She took me to a new bar-and-grill off Route 95, paneled in rough wood and hung with flowering plants. The height of the ceiling, the odd shape of the rooms, and the strips of broken glass hung from roof to floor gave the place that hectic but tedious look of a hall of mirrors. We sat at a table covered with green felt and our drinks were served on green plaid coasters. Diane came here a lot, she said, sometimes with a girlfriend, more often with Lou.

"He takes you here?" I asked, with my usual tact.

"You don't like it."

"It's noisy," I said, although, at the moment, it wasn't noisy at all; it just felt that way. Before we could get into a tussle, the waitress appeared in a stiff, ruffly dress, cut mid-thigh, worn with fishnet stockings.

"Don't get wine," my sister said.

"Why not?"

"Because this is not a wine place," but the waitress was saying how they had Riunite, chablis, burgundy, and, she thought, maybe some Sangria.

I ordered Sangria, and Diane, sighing, asked what was on draft. Our drinks arrived before we could continue. Mine was poured into a thick goblet; chunks of pineapple, orange, and a grape, speared on a toothpick, had sunk to the bottom of the glass. "It's good," I said, sipping carefully so the fruit wouldn't tumble out on my face. Diane was watching me. "Drink your beer," I said, and she grinned—the first smile I'd seen since stepping off the plane. She gulped the beer and the grin was gone.

"Are you all right?" I asked.

"I'm fine. Are *you* all right?"

I said that I was about as good as could be expected, under the circumstances. Diane glanced at me. We'd get to my problems later, she said; didn't I want to hear about Luciano?

Nodding, I drank more of the sweet wine and this time the fruit did hit me, so I fished out the toothpick and lay the dripping mess in Diane's ashtray.

"Thanks a lot," she said. But the waitress had already returned to clean up the mess and to hand Diane a fresh ashtray. Then she wiped the sticky juice from around my glass.

"If you could keep quiet a second, I'd like to say something," Diane said, lighting a thin cigarette. "I'm getting married again." Suddenly music came on, synthesized rock booming from speakers tucked into every niche, or so it sounded. "Don't you have anything to say?" she yelled.

I took one of the long cigarettes, although I don't smoke. I had to find matches, because Diane didn't offer her lighter. Then the waitress resurfaced to present us with another ashtray. I told Diane she hadn't given me a chance; she'd sprung it on me, and now was mad because I didn't have a speech to make when I was still floored by the news.

"Floored!" she said. "Why 'floored'?"

"Why not 'floored'?" I snapped back. "How long have you known this character—three weeks?"

"I wasn't even going to tell you, Mary Jo. Now I'm sorry I did."

I blew my top; I yelled and she yelled back. How predictable I was, a snob, she said, and how sick I made her, and I said how typical of her to find a noisy dump like this to have a conversation in—*and* to waste her life, I wanted to say, on another jerk. I had always been a cold fish, she was starting to say, when the waitress returned to offer us another round. "Yes," we said in unison.

"Why are you so wrought up?" Diane said, when the waitress left.

I didn't bother to answer.

"Well, put a lid on it," she said, in the older-sister tone, the one I often used on her. We were twins, born a few minutes apart, and my mother would never say—in a way we could believe—who'd come first.

"Tell me about this Luciano," I said.

And so she did, but it wasn't what I'd expected. He was the first man she could trust, the first she truly respected. "You respected *your* husband," she said, defensively. "At least that's what you told people."

I was divorced, but yes, I said that at one time I could respect David, but was that a good enough reason to get married? That had been my mistake—we both knew it—but Diane often felt that my mistakes were worth repeating. She could talk to Lou, she went on; they liked doing things together, and he was kind. Diane sounded bored, and I wondered if she was marrying just to (as our grandmother would say) "break the monotony." That was a pet phrase in our house. Nana used it as a way to wedge herself into any little trip my mother happened to be planning. It made no difference whether my mother was driving to the bank, the gas station, or to see the foot doctor. Eager for the ride, my grandmother would refer to the monotony of her stay-at-home life, as if my mother— who'd slipped off to work as soon as Nana moved in—needed the reminder. We were a family of escape artists and we'd gotten it from Nana, although she'd only been married once, to a foreigner, who—after her family had disowned her, and before my mother was born—had died.

I knew that Diane would be comparing Luciano to her first husband, Allen Graves. Born in the north of England, Allen was an athlete, heavyset and sexy, addicted to rugby. Diane had spent her married weekends at day-long rugby games and picnics and her evenings at postgame parties. She went away in the summer to England and Wales for rugby matches there; she spent at least a hundred crazed hours in emergency rooms all over the state, while Allen's smashed legs, arms, ribs—and, once, even his head—were iced, wrapped, set, and plastered. After three years of rugby, and very little else, Diane divorced Allen and not long after, the player— who'd worked at my father's plant until he was fired for absenteeism— repatriated, and Diane hardly heard from him again: a Christmas card the first year, and nothing after. Through the grapevine she learned that he had remarried and become a printer's apprentice. She also heard that his wife, an Irish schoolteacher, was expecting their first child. Diane had asked for the divorce, but was still shocked, my mother told me, at how Allen "leapt at the chance" to be free. And the day they had to go to the courthouse, she was "devastated." They cried together—my mother and Diane—when the Graves family trouped out of the courtroom without so much as a goodbye. (Yes, that was true, Diane admitted, but our mother didn't seem to recall her own remark—made as the dashing sportsman exited the hearing with no crutches or injuries to hobble his stride—that "poor" Diane would never find another one like that!)

This sounded like my mother, candid to a fault. Besides, she herself was fond of Allen, and never passed up the chance to pat the footballer's hairy hand or squeeze his muscular arm. To Diane, she might call him "the bum" or "the birdbrain," but she bought Allen extravagant Christmas presents, spending more time and cash on jackets and sweaters for the rugged son-in-law than she ever did on any of us, my father included.

Why had Diane married him? was a question no one had to ask, so clear it was that Diane, too, adored him—probably still did. They'd married, I thought at the time, for love—because they had nothing else in common. Maureen, our older sister, as fixated as our mother was on Allen, found a clump of girlie magazines in their apartment, and claimed that Allen had "sex on the brain." I'd not seen one porno magazine, I informed Maureen; and even if he *did* buy them, what did it prove? "Ask Di, why don't you?" Maureen had smirked.

But I would never ask Di; between us, touchy subjects never came up. It was Maureen—with no husbands and twenty of her forty years spent in the convent—who had sex on the brain, "for whatever good it ever did her," as Diane (who detested "Maw") liked to say. "If she ever got any, she'd see in a second just what it is, and what it isn't."

Maureen did have the occasional date, with a schoolteacher she worked with, and once with a retired policeman who lived in her building, but she didn't go out often, and never for long with one man. ("What does *that* tell you?" Diane had sneered.) Ten years our senior, Maureen seemed closer to our parents' generation, and it was hard, my mother pointed out, to find a man single and old enough. If "our Diane" had trouble, my mother said, keeping a man happy, how would "poor Maureen" ever do it? But the problem wasn't just Maw's. Nothing we learned at home, or from the nuns, proved helpful. We were slow growing up, reluctant— even though Di had had boyfriends since grade 6, and was never without one—to pull ourselves out of a stifling youth, tedious and virginal. Why was this? we were forever asking ourselves. The real problem, I'd explained to Diane long after her divorce, was that we weren't that interested in men—we just wanted to get out of the house. She laughed at that one. "Let's not talk about it, Mary Jo," she said. "Too depressing."

But now we *were* out, I was thinking as we finished our second drinks, and wondering what difference it made. Diane had promised to tell all about Luciano, but now she didn't want to: talk could spoil it. When I asked what he looked like, she merely said, "You'll meet him," then added maybe not *this* visit. She shot me a look, but it had been years since we'd specialized in stealing each other's boyfriends. Just the thought of it, though, electrified the air around us. When things settled, she asked me if I was ever going to get remarried, or if I was still allergic. I told her about a guy I'd been dating, different from my usual schmoes and dorks. "This one," I said, "is more of a rat."

"What kind of rat?" she asked, pretending not to understand.

"Like Allen," I said.

"Get out!" she said, suddenly interested.

I told her he was in medicine, but not a doctor. He wanted to make more money than a doctor, so he was in biotechnology, making life out of chemicals.

"Oh."

He wasn't yet good enough at the moneymaking end, I said, so he planned to enroll in business school to sharpen his edge. "And when he goes," I continued, "I'll never hear from him again."

"Really? Why?"

"He's thinking ahead," I said. "I'm too ordinary for him—and for his career."

"You're not ordinary, Mary Jo," she jeered. "That's something no one could ever accuse you of."

I laughed because it wasn't meant as a compliment. "He wants to make his first million before he hits 25."

"How young *is* he?" she shrieked.

"I don't know—22 or 23."

She looked away. "Why, Mary Jo? Or should I ask?"

I closed my eyes, because I didn't want to ponder, then to express this man's powerful attractions while my sister's eyes were raking my face. (Of the two of us, Diane is better-looking, and sometimes she made me feel like Maureen.) "This guy," I said, starting slowly, in a sobbing voice, "is *so*—." But I couldn't find the perfect word, and I didn't want to start blabbing. "He has to fight them off, Diane."

She stubbed out her cigarette. "That's your type," she said. "You love to suffer."

"I don't love to suffer," I said. "If I attract a hunky guy, it isn't because I love to suffer."

She lifted the glass and sloshed beer over her chin. "I'm getting drunk. Why don't we order. The food's good here. It *is*, Mary Jo."

"So," I said, changing the subject, "what does this Luciano look like?"

"It isn't Lu-shanno. *Looch*-ahno. And you know how Ma says it? Lucy-anno."

I looked up from the surface of my drink to see Diane's eyes boring into me. "I haven't gotten this worked up in an age," she said. "Not since you were home last, in fact. Remember? That was the time you told me how Allen was wiping the floor with me. I'll never forget that. Do we think we could order, Mary Jo? I'm getting drunk."

After we ordered, Diane thawed out a little. She was willing to speak of the wedding, her dress, the plans and arrangements made to introduce Dad to Luciano. "He hasn't met him?" I screamed.

"This is my last chance, Mary Jo," she said. "Don't blow it."

"Okay," I said.

"I mean it," she said, in the same tone.

The food arrived in stages. We ate in silence for a few minutes, but then started to laugh at the things we usually laughed at, because—apart from what I've already mentioned—we had everything else in common.

The waitress returned. "Are you related?" she asked. "Those two guys over there," she said, pointing to youngish men in feed caps, who saluted us from the bar, "thought you might be sisters."

"I'm the mother," I said. I waved to the feedcaps, but we didn't accept refills from them. The waitress complimented me on how young I looked, and I thanked her. The boys eventually swiveled back on their stools to face the cute barmaid, whose uniform was even briefer than our waitress's.

"Imagine!" Diane said, still gawking.

"Just like old times," I said.

The wedding was small. My father was able to come in his wheelchair. In a triple-bypass operation the doctors had done something that left both his legs paralyzed. My mother wheeled him down the makeshift aisle to the first row of folding chairs, facing the bay windows. The central window was banked with vases of lilies and roses. Outside were the rolling meadows of the golf course, deep in snow and blinding under a faultless winter sky. It was only a few degrees above zero, and a knife-like wind sheared the white powder, twirling it in gusts. When the wind calmed, the snow looked like gold enamel. Right before the ceremony, the sun dropped behind the clubhouse, turning the glittery golf course blue, striped—from the flagpole and pine trees—with violet shadows. Then someone turned on the lights and the windows went dark.

Diane was dressing in the women's lockerroom. She'd carried in her wedding suit and a vanity case filled with cosmetic jars and electric curlers. I found her sitting in front of a long mirror, while my mother rolled her hair on the heated rods. Diane had a powder puff in one hand and a mascara wand in the other, but held herself perfectly still while my mother's fumbly fingers curled the last strands of hair and drove in the pins.

Bringing her face close to a magnifying mirror propped on the ledge, Diane powdered her eyelids, brushed off the loose particles, then drew the mascara wand over the pale lashes. "Ma!" she suddenly hissed. "I'm burning."

Confused for only a second, my mother quickly pulled out pins and let the hot curling rods fall to the floor. Diane looked waxen under the strong lights, and now her head gleamed with glossy curls. My mother started brushing them out, but Diane grabbed the brush. "I'll do it! Can someone get my suit, please?" she said. "And my nylons are in the bag."

Diane was in her party mood, grim and dictatorial—a powderkeg. Her eyes caught mine in the mirror. "What are *you* doing here? I thought you were helping people find their seats." I came closer to the dressing table. "Can *you* at least find my stockings?" she said. "Here," she added, handing me the vanity case. "They're in here."

We worked on Diane together, trying not to make matters worse. My mother and I were silent, then talked together, interrupting each other, lapsing back into silence. Then Maureen was in there, too. She planked herself on the bench and started fixing her own hair with Diane's brush— which my mother snatched back, scolding Maureen, 40, for being a pest and making everybody crazy. "Go out there," Diane ordered—her first words in a quarter of an hour—"and bring the judge in. Tell him I'm ready."

She was ready. Gazing into the mirror, there she was, a bride, in beige and rose satin, her pretty face expertly outlined and shaded, lilies and roses, as my grandmother would say—but with eyes cast down, as she rummaged in her satin bag for the jeweler's boxes—one for Luciano, one a remembrance for my father. She was opening the box with the wedding ring when Mother's anxious eyes met mine. Suddenly Diane glanced up, and glared, first at my mother, then at me. "Are you two wishing me luck? Why do you have that look on your face?"

"Me?" I said.

"I wasn't talking to you," she snapped. But our mother, turning away, was already sifting through the pile of clothes and plastic bags on the bench, lifting out her purse and mine. "If I'm bothering you, Diane," she said quietly, "I can leave."

"Ma, I'm sorry," Diane replied, still looking in the mirror.

"Don't worry about it," my mother returned blandly.

The door opened and we could hear people talking, and the fainter sounds of music. Maureen had the judge by the arm. He was presented to my mother, to the bride, and then given his envelope of cash. Diane asked him to say Luciano's name, then corrected his pronunciation. Too rude, my mother must have thought, because she whisked him right out the door, thanking him for being so good as to come out on such a bitter cold day.

Maureen lingered, fluttering around Diane, and Diane received her attentions—tugs to the hem of her skirt and swipes at her shoulders—with forbearance. Maureen then kissed her sister on the cheek, leaving a lipstick smudge that she rubbed with her thumb.

"Maureen," Diane said, pulling away from the hand, "make sure you help Dad back to his place. Don't let Ma do it. *You* do it. Can you remember that?"

Glad to be of use, Maureen said she'd do anything, and soon she too was gone, leaving the bride and her matron of honor with a minute to steel ourselves for the fifty pairs of eyes that would sweep over us, focusing on our slightly different faces just starting to age, my rail-thin body in green, and Diane's fuller one in ivory and rose, the way we walked, held ourselves, and whether—this was a tough call, but people would make it anyway—she had picked the right one at last. Diane squeezed my hand in her gloved hand, and told me I was "next," in that creepy voice she used when we were little and lined up for polio shots. There was a knock on the door, and so quickly were we hustled out that traces of laughter were still on our faces when we looked out at the even rows of family and friends. I led Diane to the spot between my father in his chair and Luciano, and left her there.

And the marriage turned out (knock on wood) to be happy. Diane is pregnant with her second child. She and Luciano have built a house so big that they're broke and Diane has years to shop in flea markets and bargain basements to fill the empty rooms to her taste. She takes that kind of long view now. She stayed home to enjoy her daughter's childhood, and even let my mother in on some of it, especially now that my mother is retired and alone, with time—and its monotony—on her hands. Very few of the people in this picture I took, after walking Diane up that short aisle, are still with us. My father died within the year of a heart attack, and our favorite uncle went out suddenly and painfully not two years after the wedding. My mother and aunt, sisters, had married best friends, my father and uncle. Having made exactly the kind of marriage Diane and I tried so hard to avoid, the sisters seemed, nonetheless, to miss the love and company of their mates. I was struck by this, but what did it mean but that time softens all blows.

I'm married now, too, and not to the phony doctor, who's long gone. Diane came to my wedding in City Hall, and met my husband on the spot, but still with enough time to evaluate the kind of insurance I was taking out against the tedium. I saw—as she entered the dreary, soot-colored room that was to be my wedding chapel, with its scarred wood counter and dusty, barred windows—how her eyes swept past me to rest on my husband-to-be, taking in his wide, gold-skinned face, his narrow eyes and pencil mustache, the startled look he has—bred so deeply into his culture—when faced with the pale-skinned, blue-eyed devil. His face warmed up, though, when he saw that I really did have a prettier double, and for once I didn't mind Diane stealing the show. Our turn came, and Hiro and I faced the tired-looking matron, elbow-deep in documents, who was to lead us in our exchange of civil vows. I felt Diane's hand on one side, pinching my arm, and Hiro's on the other, cool and loose.

We were man and wife, brother-in-law and sister as we strode out into the lurid city night with its screeching cars and honking horns. Hiro was in the middle of the street, flagging down cabs, when Diane hissed into my ear: "Mary Jo—*a Chinaman?*"

I said that Hiro was not Chinese, but she repeated it, a grin stretched across her rosy face, a look of exaltation.

In the course of time, I explained to my family that Hiro was not as exotic as he might seem. Born in this country, he was not "a Chinaman," as my father would have called him. Still, we had nothing at all in common, not in this life, nor—if we chose to fall back on what we'd been taught—in the next. There was a thick buffer of strangeness between us—much better, I thought, than a hope chest full of towels.

After the wedding dinner, I hugged Diane and Hiro hugged Diane, Hiro kissed Diane and I kissed Diane, then Diane left to catch a cab to the airport and to the family waiting for her at home, and Hiro and I sat in the glassy bar of our hotel, holding hands, grinning at each other, eager in the first few minutes of our marriage for the long free fall.

Poor Richard

Richard Parkinghouse, a registered pharmacist, hired a schoolgirl to vend cigarettes and make sodas for his customers, then stood behind a wall of white Parke-Davis cartons and tried to guess her experience. She had thick bangs and a sulky look. She wore glasses. She drank what was left at the bottom of the metal milkshake mixers. She blushed when she made change. When there weren't any customers, she didn't like to dust the shelves with the feather duster. She said (when he asked) that she owned a white dress, but the waitress uniform she wore the next week was too skimpy, so he offered ("I have all my girls wear them") one of his white coats. Then he went back behind the counter and leaned his elbows on the glass shelf.

Her feet hurt—he could see that. She had on a pair of scuffed black flats with pointed toes, and no stockings, and there was no place to sit behind the fountain. Once, when he'd come over for a glass of water, he saw that she had slipped out of the shoes, her heels on the toes, toes on the cool floor. The feet were red. That first night, the regular customers came by, all volunteer firemen; some of them tried to start up a conversation. She was polite. They looked when she turned around to use the milkshake machine. The uniform was tight across her back. (When she finally got the lab coat from him, that looked tight, too.)

It was warm that first night. After nine o'clock there weren't many customers. He came around his counter and told her she could make anything she wanted for herself. Then he went to count the money and found a candy wrapper next to the cash register; he said he didn't want her leaving papers around like that.

"Tired?" he asked, returning to the soda fountain. She said no. "I can tell you're tired," he said, then told her that he lived not too far from her neighborhood and would drop her home. They didn't talk on the way there, but before she got out of his car, a blue Chevy, he said he'd have her white coat laundered with his once a week, and not to worry about it. "Goodnight now," he said, and watched her walk up the back porch steps. Only the bathroom light was on.

57

Mary Gilfillan was eleven when the family moved to Fairview Street, the first house they owned that had a pulley line. Her mother could hang wash from the entry window, standing among the empty bottles, with the clothespin bag hung on the windowsill. When they first moved in, her mother did a wash every day, just for the fun of it. She had a big wicker basket all the kids tried to flop in when it was filled with clean sheets.

The house had two floors, eight small square rooms, and French doors separating the parlor from the den, and the den from the dining room. Her mother had two copper planters to hang on one set of doors, but the other doors stayed bare. The parlor was reserved for company, the dining room for holidays, and the TV—a floor model with a maroon set of rabbit ears—was put in the den. Mary's mother bought a new set of print slipcovers for the couch and armchair, but they kept their old black hassock and the pale green rug that had covered the parlor floor in the Linden Street tenement. They were still calling it "the new house" when Mary was thirteen, and her father had removed the gingerbread shutters and applied a coat of charcoal-gray paint to the yellow clapboards, and a coat of glossy red to cover the brick foundation. Her mother had strung up a second clothesline from the porch to the garage window, but just a single line, no pulley. She had to go out and buy an aluminum pole with a notch at one end to hold the line up. There was another baby and more laundry.

It was around that time that Jim Ryan's son-in-law left the old drugstore on the avenue to buy his own, north of the city. Richard's drugstore was bigger, newer than Ryan's, but it had a lot less in it. He sold cigarettes and "coffee cabinets" to the firehouse, but his drug business wasn't anywhere near as good as his father-in-law's. Richard had married the Ryans' middle daughter, Eileen, a black-haired girl with a fresh face. There was only one grandchild, Michael Francis, in the third grade at St. Ray's. People in the neighborhood knew the store wasn't doing very well; when they stepped into Ryan's for a card or a vanilla Coke, they always asked. Lila St. Paul, the clerk who sold stamps and took gas and electric payments, knew the Ryans well, and few conversations ended without Miss St. Paul saying how sorry she felt for Richard and poor Eileen. People knew she probably exaggerated, but even Big Jim had to admit—if you could get him on the subject—that the location wasn't everything his son-in-law had hoped for. In fact, there was talk of Richard's closing down, but somehow this talk never seemed to come to anything. Why doesn't he come back in with you? people wanted to ask. But you got the idea, just being in Ryan's, with the greeting cards jammed in with the toys and shampoo, that it wasn't likely. Big Jim and Richard were too different. People sometimes took a ride up to North Providence just to see how the new place was doing. It was bright and airy, but the shelves were thinly stocked; there was a single row of cotton balls, for instance, and a solitary box of rubber gloves; even the magazine rack was bare-looking. People loved to tell you that he had fewer flavors of ice cream than Ryan's, and Ryan's was not really an ice cream place. People blamed it on Richard's personality: he was too stiff.

Mary didn't know that Mr. Parkinghouse was always looking at her from behind his counter, but she did know that, among his magazines, there was a copy of a book called *The Sane Science of Sex*. She was afraid to look into it. He might come in the back way. He had gone out to get a meatball sandwich for supper. There were a lot of magazines and books behind his counter, stacked on a carton near the stool where he made up prescriptions. He had a transistor radio back there, too, and a pair of high-top sneakers. One night when he was driving her home, he said that he was interested in child psychology.

He was a medium-sized man with a brush cut and heavy glasses in black frames; he never smiled. People said it was from being married to Eileen Ryan, who talked all the time. Mary figured he just liked to read; in fact, he spent most of his time at the drugstore, Monday through Saturday, reading behind the counter. He was always complaining about money, yet people in the old neighborhood said he wasn't really interested in money. They wanted to know from her what he was like, but she couldn't tell them. Everything she said was vague. It's too bad about Mr. Parkinghouse's store, they'd say. She'd say that he was easy to work for, as long as you looked busy when there were no customers. She never told anyone about his offering to have a coat laundered for her every week. If she told them that, they might understand that he was kind, and not the cold fish people thought. The fact was, she really didn't like him either.

When they moved to the new house, Mary stood at each window gazing out. She didn't want to forget the way it looked the first time. She liked the idea that the neighborhood was mostly one-family houses with lawns and cement walks. It wasn't like the last neighborhood, full of triple-deckers with dirt sidewalks, weeds, and unpaved driveways. She thought, in the beginning, that every time she opened the new front door, or stood in the hallway staring at herself in the full-length mirror, she would feel the newness. But that sensation soon wore off. There was a streetlight outside her bedroom window, the old-fashioned kind with a fluted metal cap that dropped a bowl of light on the sidewalk. Her other window opened onto old Miss Mulligan's bedroom. Miss Mulligan had kept house for her brother, who died years ago of a heart attack, then she stayed on alone. On the other side of the house was an Italian family; they spoke no English at all. Through the front windows were all Irish families, except for the two Mahoney sisters, who lived on the first floor of the street's only tenement, which they owned. Through the front door was a pair of red maples; through the kitchen windows, a lilac bush, three evenly spaced pine trees, and the parlor windows of the Italian family's house; the parlor was painted yellow-gold. You couldn't see anything in the Mulligan house because the old lady kept the shades pulled at all times. The dining room and den windows looked out on a young Irish couple, trying—Mary had heard the wife tell her mother—to have a baby. She liked to kneel by that window and lean her chin on the sill, peeking through the Venetian blinds, but nothing was ever happening.

Mr. Parkinghouse, 36, lived in the suburbs and was a member of St. Ray's Rosary and Altar Society, although not active. He had gone to Sacred Heart College right in the city, majoring in chemistry. His father had wanted him to be a doctor. During junior year, he'd clerked—labeling bottles and keeping accounts—at Ryan's, where he met Eileen, who worked the soda fountain. When he graduated, they got married; then he became a pharmacist. Everybody expected him to stay at Ryan's; there was enough business for two, and Big Jim was getting on. But not five years after his marriage, the son-in-law bought the doughnut-shop premises in North Providence. Mr. Ryan was forced to go back to work full-time, even though his wife was ailing. It was a shame, people thought, now—when Richard's business was ailing too—more than ever. There was a rift going way back between Richard and his mother-in-law, but people could only guess what that was all about. The other two Ryan girls, Pat and Dotty, had married the O'Connor brothers, who worked in the A&P, where their father was manager. They could have done better, was the general opinion, although—unlike their father—neither girl had gone beyond high school.

Richard Parkinghouse, who considered himself "free and independent," as he put it, of the Ryans, and of the neighborhood where he'd grown up and where his new girl lived, had had three employees to work the fountain. The first had married a volunteer fireman after she'd gotten pregnant, dropping out of college in her sophomore year. The boy she married hadn't gone to college at all; he became a professional fireman in the city, after they moved there. His second girl, the first girl's sister, had also met a fireman, but she hadn't married him. She left the pharmacy when she graduated from high, and got a job at the telephone company. She was still going out with the boy from the firehouse, but it was an on-

and-off thing. Both of these girls had been ideal fountain clerks, attracting business without looking cheap. Rosy and well-fed, with sturdy legs, they had clear complexions and straight teeth. They didn't have about them that air that girls often have who work the fountain at sixteen. The latest one, Mary Gilfillan, was a different story. She wasn't that friendly; she didn't seem to like the work. Because of bad skin and the makeup she wore to cover it, she didn't give a wholesome impression, and the firehouse didn't take to her. But *he* did. He enjoyed the Saturday nights; she was one of the few people he liked talking to. Mostly he complained. He knew that, at the end of the night, she went home downhearted, but she was glum by nature. She was an odd duck, babyish and old-looking at the same time. They were a lot alike, he thought, although sometimes that made him harder on her. He nagged her about dusting, and about cleaning the milkshake machine between customers; she was the type of girl who needed to be told a thing over and over. She was slow-moving, and often careless with the orders. She didn't like waiting on customers, yet he kept her on. Sometimes they didn't say one word to each other all night, then they'd talk for half an hour sitting in the car out in front of her house. She seemed to like the conversations.

He didn't know that her father was waiting up. Without turning on a light, she'd sneak up the stairs, stopping to listen for breathing. Once he called her into his bedroom. She explained that some school friends had come by the drugstore and offered her a ride home. They stopped for a Coke on the way: that's why she was late. He didn't believe it. He turned over in bed to face the wall. He would say no more, so Mary crept to her room in the dark.

In the winter, her mother had another baby, and Mary stayed home part of every Saturday to help with the work and take care of the younger ones, but her mother didn't see why she should have to quit her job; the little pocket money came in handy. Every Monday her father took her paycheck to the bank with his and cashed them both. "How much of this do you want back?" he always teased. "Dollar enough?" Then, when he got home, he would give her the envelope so she could count it.

One week she announced that she would cash her own check. She asked her mother to tell him. Her mother, looking up with a diaper pin in her mouth and a hand around the baby's middle, said to tell him herself. "You know how much he likes doing that."

"I need the money to go downtown early Monday," she told her father, "so I'm going to the bank myself."

He was in a good mood and just shook his newspaper in response. Later—as her mother had said he would—he took it out on her at the dinner table. There was no conversation, and Mary got a look every time she tried to start one.

The next week, her father, who had asked pleasantly enough on Monday whether she thought he was cheating her, didn't ask to cash the drugstore check, but she knew he was waiting. There was no check that week; there had been none the week before, and she knew that pretty soon she'd have to quit.

Mr. Parkinghouse's mood had changed and everybody knew it. On Tuesday, he closed up shop early, drove down to Ryan's, ate an ice-cream sundae and drank a Coke at his father-in-law's counter. Mr. Ryan, who had had a bad night with Helen, didn't know what to make of it. He left his drug cubby and whisked over to the fountain, sending his girl off to dust cards. The father-in-law picked up the dish towel and started wiping the counter, waiting for his son-in-law to break the ice. Ryan hadn't "laid eyes" on his daughter's husband in over a month. Eileen hadn't called home, but his wife had called Eileen, and they had discussed Mikey's report card—better than usual—and Mrs. Ryan had passed on the news about one of Eileen's chums who had gone into the convent. For want of something better to say—and although he didn't know the girl personally—he was prepared to pass on the "tidbit" to Richard, but Richard didn't have the courtesy to look up from his bowl. He ate the sundae with the long Coke spoon, then drank his Coke without using the straw. Ryan thought he could use a haircut. Richard, although he was thinking about other things, noticed the counter was sticky and dabbed with ice cream, even though the old man had been slapping at it for the past five minutes.

Mr. Parkinghouse had come in to try and get his girl a job, but he left the drugstore without even asking. "How's the family?" Ryan had finally said, hands on his hips and the rag hanging over his shoulder. "Fine," Richard answered, but it was clear he didn't want to get into it. Mr. Ryan turned on his heel and marched back to his cubby. He had had it up to the gullet with that bum. He dialed home, but the line was busy. Miss St. Paul could hear—the bell over the door had rung as Mr. Parkinghouse exited—the old druggist cursing and swearing in the back of the store. "He's pushing a heart attack," she said in a loud whisper, "with that attitude."

"You can say that again," John the barber said. He had just stepped in—the bell ringing behind him—for a coffee.

Two weeks later, Mary was let go. Her father had not gotten over the business with the checks, but her mother had figured it out the second time it happened, and told her daughter she was letting that guy walk all over her. "I suppose you expect *I'll* give you the money!" she said. "Well, you couldn't be more wrong, my girl." But she did give Mary five dollars, then another dollar on Saturday—to keep her in stockings, as she put it. "Now *I'm* broke," she said, holding her wallet open so her daughter could see how empty it was.

Wearing the lab coat that hadn't once been sent to the laundry, Mary told Richard Parkinghouse that she was sorry to see the store close. She spoke to him like a customer, over the wall of medicines and through the glass barrier. She had to look up to talk, and she could see him staring back; that, plus the way the overhead light made two balloons of his glasses, made her feel like laughing, and she couldn't finish what she was trying to say. She took a folded pink tissue out of her pocket and blew her nose.

"It looks empty tonight, doesn't it?" he said.

She turned to look. Even the cigarette and candy counters—their best business—were looking thin. A week ago she might have asked him why he didn't reorder, but lately he hadn't even been putting on his lab coat; he had taken both of his coats home one night and never brought them back, so she didn't ask. There were hardly any customers the last few weeks; he sat from 6 till closing with a paperback book open on the high counter. He didn't even hound her about the dusting, and she—of her own free will—made an effort to cater to the firemen, smiling and wiping the counter while they smoked and drank their Cokes. (The firemen, right to the end, came over on their breaks.)

Those last weeks, he often closed early, driving his girl home a little after eight. Sometimes they stopped at Dunkin Donuts on the way. He rarely talked about anything personal, but one time he told her he thought he had once had a vocation to the priesthood, and asked if she'd ever considered giving her life to God. She thought she *did* have a vocation, she told him, then began to talk of friends who were already postulants, but he didn't seem at all interested in the specifics. He did ask if she'd care for another jelly donut, then told her she shouldn't eat things like that, with her skin. That was embarrassing—he could see—but it was too late to take it back.

"What do you use on your face?" he asked, pouring cream into his second cup of coffee. She asked him what he'd recommend, and he paused, looked in the mirror behind the counter, studying the face clouded with medicated makeup, brown hollows under the eyes, mouth folded down at the corners, and wished he hadn't brought it up. He didn't want to raise hopes, and this had lasted long enough; the store was very nearly in the hands of the bank. She was looking in the mirror, too, and he could see she was still waiting for the advice. "I'll give you some stuff next time," he said. "Don't worry about it."

It was a cloudless winter day—fresh snow covered the ground—when he closed up shop. They unrolled a paper banner ("Gone Out Of Business") to hang across the plate-glass window, with the number of Ryan's Drugs underneath, a courtesy for the regular customers, who could go right back to where they started. A few had been loyal to Richard right up to the end—he was quiet, but a real gentleman, the ones who liked him said. Mary had put on her new black Granny boots, bought with the overdue wages paid up in full the day before. She'd said he didn't have to, but he told her to take it while he had it to give. She showed the check to her mother, and Mr. Gilfillan himself took it down to the bank. "You're lucky to see any of this" was all he said. "That guy's in hock up to his eyeballs." Her mother told him to lay off the girl, and, surprisingly enough, he did. He went out the door and returned with the cash envelope, plus a quart of peppermint stick ice cream he had picked up at Ryan's. "He'd never do that for me!" Mrs. Gilfillan told her daughter, so the husband could hear.

Mr. Parkinghouse complimented her on the sharp boots and gave her a boxful of "soap samples" to make up for not recommending an acne cream like he said he would. She shook his hand, although she was sure to see him again, and soon—he was going back to Ryan's, but her mother said she still couldn't picture it. Mr. Parkinghouse held her hand loosely, gave it a squeeze, then bent over to pull out the second pair of shoes she kept under the counter, and handed her the bag. The counter was covered with brown paper and all the shelves were empty. The cash register was gone, the fountain machines sold. He unlocked the door and locked it again after she went out, but he didn't wave—although he was standing right there—when she turned back at the curb, squinting in the glare of the snow. It was hard to see, but she could see he wasn't waving. And anyway, the bus was coming and she had to fumble fast for change.

On the bus she opened his box and found two sample jars of cold cream, some bottles of Kaopectate and aspirin, a roll of Tums, a pair of taupe stockings, four five-cent packages of white tissues, and a few rolls of Lifesavers. On the bottom of the box was a card with a pink rose on the outside and plain on the inside: "To My Helper," he had written: "A Friend Always."

"What'd he give you?" her mother asked, the minute she was in the door. "Did he give you something?"

But Mary—who had pitched it all (except for the tissues and the candy, which fit into her pocketbook), and was *still* embarrassed—said no.

Every Hour That Goes By Grows Younger

When Margery arrived at the office, her boss had already made his own coffee and was drinking it out of the new cup and saucer, blue and white china. His desk was immaculate. A single paper was on it, and the paperweight, a brass car. She had seen these brass cars given as bingo prizes at Rocky Point and Crescent Park, which is where he'd gotten his. She'd entered his office to water the one plant, snake plant, that sucked in all the water she gave it, and its dirt was still dry. She was on her way— "Mrs. DiBellis?"—to refill the watering can, but turned back.

"What time do you have?"

"Quarter past nine," she replied, then walked into her own office. She wanted to ask if his watch had stopped, but that wasn't why he'd asked. For all that he had his own key and could operate the electric coffee machine just as well as she could (it only took a minute, and everything was laid out for him—a baby could do it!), Mr. Galucci preferred that his secretary arrive at nine sharp. Margery tried, but it wasn't that easy.

She sat down at her all-white desk and dialed her mother's work number. Nothing was new at home. The sister in Washington State had gotten half a dozen pink roses for Valentine's Day. This was a good sign. Margery's father was bored at home, yet not bored enough to do the few simple chores her mother wrote down for him on the shopping pad before leaving for work at six-thirty, quarter to seven. If he'd "just do the few things, he'd feel better, don't you think? He needs to keep busy."

Margery thought her father needed an outside interest; laundry, dishes, and cleaning out the bedroom closets were not—although she didn't tell her mother this—going to pull him out of a depression he'd been in (she'd never say this either) all his life. Her mother wouldn't want to hear it. Margery asked about Charlie and Mary Ann, the oldest and youngest. The mother didn't know, they never called. "Do they ever call *you*?"

No, they never called her—why should they? Her mother said she didn't have time to chat: the work was piled up on her desk.

It was 9:35. Margery opened her desk drawer and took out a compact and lipstick. In the mirror her lipstick was already perfect, but she lay-

ered it with an extra coat of Lilac Summer, then got up to use the ladies'
room. Mr. Galucci was still on the phone. That was his button lit up.
Now he was off the phone, but still quiet in there so early on a Monday
morning.

No one was in the ladies' room, so Margery looked at herself, front
and back, in the full-length mirror: her stockings were a little dark for the
taupe linen (a dress for spring, although still bitter cold outside). Then
she sank into a lounge chair. The morning paper, folded into a quarter,
lay on the footrest, but she didn't pick it up. She put her head back and
closed her eyes.

It didn't help. Closing her eyes made it worse, so she opened them.
Outside the streaky bathroom windows was a bright cold day; a big
square of light fell on the green linoleum. This made it worse, so she
folded up her legs and arranged her dress loosely around them. It was
bad enough to feel sick without being squeezed by pantyhose and pant-
ies, a tight waistband and a buttoned jacket. Her stomach was so tender,
she could feel the blouse buttons pressing little dull circles on her skin.
She couldn't stay in the bathroom all day; besides, who would want to?

Mr. Galucci had placed a note on her desk. She could see that he
wasn't in his office, so he must be sitting in Mr. Hargreaves's office, to get
the estimates of last week's sales, and to give his impressions. Margery
slipped off her brown suede pumps and curled her toes around the bar at
the back of the desk. She felt like resting a minute, but instead she read
the note. "Where *are* you?" it said. "I had to get my own client files for
Mr. H. I didn't find them till the last minute"—it was a long note—"and
then I was late. Your husband called and said to call back at the office.
B.G."

Margery was starting to pick up the receiver, when the phone rang.
"Fire, house, and car," she said in even tones.

"Mrs. DiBellis?"

"Speaking."

"This is Dr. Maher."

Just that morning, after a hard night in the pitch-dark bedroom (Stephen
liked every double shade pulled to the sill and fitted into the window
hollow, so no morning light could seep in and spot the wall or the floor),
she had heard the glass clock in the living room chime 2 and then 3. Then
she must have dozed, because next she heard 5 chime and then 6. When it
was time to get up, the pain seemed to have moved. She lay there—the
bed felt lumpy and the parts of her touching it felt sore and hot—but the
usual pain, the pain she'd been feeling since Christmas, had spread itself
out—it wasn't all concentrated in the stomach and sides.

Margery stood in her long, wrinkled nightie on the cold bathroom tiles. The hot water was running in the sink with a bar of soap over the drain making a nice soapy steam. (The bathroom smelled bad, musty, but this helped.) She switched on the wall heater and sat on the toilet to cut her toenails, which felt long. But the minute she lifted her foot to snip her big toenail with a special pair of clippers that worked so well they were always a pleasure to use (and so few things were like that), the pain came back, worse. She put the clippers down. The heat was pouring in from the wall and it was hard to breathe this air so hot and steamy, oily with soap suds. She turned the machine off, and put the soap cake back in its dish. The blue bubbles around the drain washed right down, but there was a soap curd that she didn't bother to wipe (let it harden). That's what the pain felt like—a salted crust on the smooth inside of the stomach, and eating like acid into the red walls.

One of the troubles with this—or any—pain was how easy it was to visualize, which made it worse and added nausea. She was reading on the bottom of the tissue box an offer for a plexiglas toothpaste holder that would squeeze the toothpaste from the bottom, and that also had slots for the brushes. She reached into the cabinet to see if the unopened box had the same offer. No: a different kind of tissue. If she could only be sure to clip this offer when (she wedged her hand into the side of the box to estimate the thickness) they used these up. She could never remember a thing like this, but if she clipped the offer now, when she thought of it, the tissues might get wet sitting on the toilet shelf, and he wouldn't like it. A red felt pen was kept in the tissue box—there for spur-of-the-moment jottings—and, fingering it out, she drew an arrow on the blue box, then rotated the box so the arrow was hidden. When she threw the box out, *she* would see it. (This was the kind of thought that could make the pain disappear completely.)

The alarm went off in the bedroom. It rang for a long time, until he pushed the orange button—which he would do three times, then get up when he always did at 7:15. Only once had she asked him why he set it at 6:30. He wasn't fully awake—his hair was all bunched up in the back and one eye weeping. He put a hand on the edge of the bed and stood, trudged to the bathroom, his feet far apart. She was staring at the bird's nest at the back of his head, when suddenly he turned:

"Margery, does it bug you that I set it early?" They had been married exactly one year, although she'd been married at least five years to someone else. "Not a bit," she told him. "I was just—."

He continued into the bathroom. While he was in there, washing and brushing, shaving, powdering and scenting, she opened the bathroom door a few times to ask him what he planned to wear that day. After closing the door, she pulled out the gray suit and light-blue shirt and hung them on the doorknob; she piled socks and underwear on the bed, pried the wooden shoe trees out of his black loafers with the tassels, and put the shoes just below the underclothes. Only once did she look at the clock: it said 7:35. So what difference did it make that he set the alarm 45 minutes early?

That morning, when Stephen came out of the steamy bathroom in his ruby terrycloth robe, he stopped at the doorway. "I didn't mean to hurt your feelings."

"They aren't hurt," she said briskly. Now she was pulling out her own clothes. Just as he was about to say more, she remembered the coffee.

"Margery," he said to her back, as she slipped by.

"What?" he heard from the kitchen.

"I like it that way. Is it something you can get used to?"

Now he was in the kitchen. She was scooping coffee out of the can—spilled a little—and swept it into the palm of her hand, then ran the water. "I don't care how you set it," she said. "It doesn't bother me." She said this in a pleasant tone, relaxed, so he padded over and put his arms around a waist that was bigger than it should be—and it hadn't always been that way. In broad daylight, under the white puffy robe, it seemed even fatter.

This kind of disagreement was trivial, wasn't it? she'd asked her friend, Alice Figueroa, Hargreaves's secretary, later that day. She should be thankful, Alice said, she had an understanding husband, and with the disposition of a peach. "If *I* talk back, or get a word in edgewise—." (Alice's Tom was a drinker, so Margery was sorry she brought it up; it *was* trivial, and now poor Alice was feeling sorry for herself, and why shouldn't she?)

The alarm went off for the second time, rang and rang. Then it stopped. She went into the kitchen and sat at the round table, the glass of the tabletop so cold she could feel the chill on both elbows right through the thick robe. On the table was a *Pennysaver,* the kind of thing to make the pain worse, reading about the types of things people had to sell and how desperate they were to get them off their hands. And why? So they could move out of town and buy all new—the exact same things for more money. This was cynical, but the pain did it.

Steve would like a better garden hose this spring—one that wasn't so stiff—so they could make a border all around the edges of the house, and put in some tomatoes in the yard—now that the old tree was cut down, and they got a little sun back there. Flipping open the yellow booklet, she was running her finger down the columns when the pain suddenly got so bad she was rocking the flimsy wrought-iron chair with yellow plastic pads. So she got up, walked gingerly into the living room, carrying the *Pennysaver* and a pencil from the telephone table.

She knew what it was. It was cancer. She even knew how long it'd been there: she got it just before the wedding, but then it felt more like a stitch. She could feel it under the beige and teal silk suit. Then it was more on the rim of the stomach, and food and liquor didn't seem to touch it. She drank champagne and ate the three-course dinner, then a second dinner when they drove to Boston. Even now she could still eat, and had had a big spaghetti dinner last night in a South County restaurant right on the water. It was their anniversary today and they'd celebrated a little in advance, but after one year, she didn't fit into her wedding suit—too tight in the skirt—so she wore a dress of her mother's (dark green and blue). They wore the same size now, so were both able to double their wardrobes, although Margery tended to borrow more things and her mother fewer. She had eaten the dinner, a real Italian dinner with separate fish and meat courses, and it had gone down okay, and stayed down, but now she could see it had been a mistake.

The cancer had woven a white net in the bowl of her stomach: she had seen something like it in an X-ray—a "mammograph," they call them. She knew it was a cancer by the strange looks of cobwebby or very fine lace massing in the stomach, foggy against a dark background. This troubled the food and made the stomach tender, so everything just sat there, undigested, and turned hard. That's what it felt like now—so hard that not even the edges were melted.

Here was a hose and a good brand, only 20 dollars, unpatched and in perfect condition. She jotted down the phone number on a lined pad left out on the coffee table in case anyone wanted to play a card game. She'd call from work, and maybe pick it up on the way home, a nice surprise.

In the first month of pain, she thought it might be a baby. She wasn't going to tell anyone, but it slipped out one day, talking to her mother about renting a cabin, the two couples, on the Cape in late September. The timing would be wrong, Margery had said. "For what?" her mother replied, "You've got vacation days coming to you."

Margery was starting to put it on Steve, but she didn't want her mother inquiring into the details of his job—which she didn't even inquire into herself—so she just spilled the beans.

"Can I tell your father? What does Stephen think? Will you be able to afford it with your mortgage payments so high? You'll have to quit playing golf, won't you? I don't want to tell the others till you're sure."

Her mother said all these things at once. Then: "Don't count on it, Margery, until you have it checked. I wouldn't even tell *him*." (I haven't, Margery said.) "Wait and take the test."

Margery let her mother talk. Although she was full of frets, she seemed to like the idea. Margery called her doctor that afternoon, but he couldn't see her until two weeks from Friday; and by then, of course, she knew it wasn't a baby.

That was the alarm again, and the bathroom door closing. No, it couldn't be the bathroom door, because here he was, still in his pajamas. "Is it paining you?" he asked.

"Take your shower. I'm all right. I just got up early. I never realized how bright this room was." They looked at the room, all blue—blue rug and blue-upholstered furniture—flooded with white light, the curtains a pure white film.

"You better take your shower so I can take mine." She had told him that ulcers ran in the family, and as a little girl she'd suffered every spring and had sometimes had to stay home from school, the pain was so intense. This was the first story she had told; now she was telling them all the time. She was surprised how quickly people would believe a story, no matter how far-fetched.

Mr. Galucci didn't come right back after his meeting, so there was time to let the doctor's message sink in. Her boss had gone to Paul's for coffee and brought Margery (he could be quite thoughtful when he was in the mood) a pineapple Danish, in a bag with a napkin, black coffee—although he'd already made a potful—a pink Sweet 'n Low envelope and two creams. This was exactly right and she thanked him, then hunted in her purse for change, but he said forget it. He was in a good mood, and sat in the reception area with a cigarette while Margery tried to eat her Danish without swallowing any of it. Mr. Galucci was just saying when he and Doris were planning to take two weeks at their camp in Maine—and maybe Margery, too, wanted that time off, and had she and her husband made their vacation plans yet?—when the phone rang, and it was for him, so Margery could wrap the Danish in its napkin and toss it in the basket under a cardboard box. She put the full coffee cup in there, too. When she sat up straight, folding her fingers smoothly together and placing them on the desk, she saw that it was—the red and black desk calendar said so clearly—the thirteenth of April, a Monday.

There was work to do before lunch: two files to put papers into—public notifications and partial payments—which she stapled into the folders. Three bills had to be made up and copied, with a percentage to look up in a book on the fifth floor; the mail opened and sorted, and she did all these things with a pain that was only a half- or quarter-ring, and dull.

One development was her fingers were all swelled and the new wedding ring buried in soft flesh. Her hands looked like mitts and they were always pink from the pressure. What pressure? She wasn't sure if it was simply getting fat, or pressure from the sickness that was spreading everywhere. She could picture so easily her insides criss-crossed with this white nest, a big swirl of threads. Buried in the finger was the thin ring, white-gold, with a pear-shaped diamond on the matching band; the two rings locked together and the diamond's head lapped over. It was a very nice set, different from what she'd worn with her first husband—a pearl and no wedding ring at all. And he hadn't gotten himself a wedding ring either, which might have been part of the problem, who knows?

When she'd lost the first husband (people put it differently, but she always worded it this way, no matter what her mother always said about blame falling on the wrong party), she gained weight—which wouldn't help, her mother said, in getting someone interested in her; if she *wanted* another husband, maybe she didn't. But that was not the problem. Men were always interested in Margery, fat or thin, and her mother knew this. In fact, she liked to brag about it when Margery wasn't there to hear.

"I'm too *fat*—is *that* what you're saying?" Margery shouted at her mother, two weeks after telling her that she and Rick were getting a divorce, and the mother could see that she meant business, the boy had moved out and Margery was home alone at night—which was really, the girl had said, no different from before, as Rick Leary had been keen on the nightlife: night sports and night drinking, and Margery Leary—fagged from getting up every morning at quarter past six to drive downtown and be on time for her job—couldn't keep up. So he went alone, although he was tired, too (close, in fact, to losing his job as, her mother would snidely say, a glorified mail boy at the *Globe*), with that long commute to and from Boston, and on so few hours sleep: it was a wonder he didn't crash the car on 95.

Margery, her mother had replied, was too fat *only* if she wanted, at 31, to land another husband, but she was not too fat for other things. "I'm not criticizing you," her mother added, "but I see the girls out there—some of these girls who work with me—and they've got everything going for them, and they're *still* sitting home Saturday nights doing hand laundry and watching TV. It's tough," her mother warned. But Margery already had dates for Saturday nights, and she'd only been single two weeks. Some men—one who had dated her sister, and whom she hadn't seen in three years—found out she was single and had already called. That, she repeated, was not the problem.

Even now—sick and heavier, pale, slow-moving and irritable—it wasn't the problem. She could tell (although she didn't tell her mother) just by the way Mr. Galucci hovered around her desk and bought her things and how the men in the building looked up from their work to chat when the ailing Margery padded down the aisles of the main office to bring papers to Mr. Hargreaves, that this was still not the problem.

The new rings—wedding and engagement—were more traditional. They did it right this time, for Stephen DiBellis had also been married before, with one child out in California, with the ex. Everything in the new marriage was done by the book. They had gone for instructions at the rectory, had a church wedding once the first marriages had been annulled (Expensive? Yes, she told Alice—but well worth it), and bought a starter home. They did things together, developed interests and hobbies in common—or rather, Margery regularly attended Red Sox, Patriots, and Friars games, went ice-fishing, played bridge, and watched X-rated movies. This was exactly the life she wanted, she told Alice, and she was working to keep it that way: it involved family, regular hours, regular sex (although she didn't highlight this point for Alice), and a lot of care and consideration. But it was all worth it. They were happy.

When Margery closed her heavy file drawer, there was one thing left to do: deliver the stock quotations to Mr. Galucci's desk—he would be gone for the rest of the morning. There was never much to do in the office because Mr. Galucci, a tidy and methodical man, liked to do his own work, and he was quick and efficient. Margery went to the ladies' room to run cold water over her swollen hands. That felt good and, since no one was in there, Margery let herself cry over the streaming water. She had one hand on the cock and when she cried hard, she turned the water on full force. Once the water splashed out of the sink, and she had to step back or be spotted.

When she finished, she turned the water off. It was nearly lunchtime and people would soon flood into the ladies' room. Margery looked at her glittery pink face—it wasn't a mess, but there were mascara streaks under the eyes. She washed her face, but had no fresh makeup to fix it up, so she left it bare. She looked young, fat but young. She returned to her desk and opened a fresh pack of Chicklets and put two tablets in her mouth and let them melt there. She didn't feel any pain; she couldn't feel it now that she knew it wasn't in there. What was in there? Nothing. There was nothing growing in there that was going to kill her. There might be stomach cramps, or a backwash of acid, yes, but nothing extra. Underneath the stomach, though, in the other place was something new that would give everybody a big surprise, when Margery decided to tell them. But she was going to wait a while, get used to the idea, enjoy it all by herself for a few days.

Two phones were ringing. She pushed a button—it was Stephen, and why hadn't she called him back? "Hold on," she said, and pushed the other button. It was her mother.

"Ma?" she said in a bright tone, all ready to shatter.

The Faithful

It had been raining steadily for four days. The air was saturated: trees, vines, and bushes crushed the islands dividing the roads and parking lots, growing a lighter green every day, silvery with water drops. It was a more beautiful and perfumed spring than he had ever seen. The air was cool, often cold, but felt soft and bloated. Even when it wasn't raining, the air was forever changing state and, chased by wind, it glistened on the skin or dribbled down a window.

Dr. Warren was resting. He sat at his desk and looked out the window at the rain-drenched bushes and wet parking lot. He was about to make his visits: one to each of the offices, exactly like this one, along the wide carpeted corridor smelling of wet paint. In each was a patient; some were in wheelchairs drawn up close to his desk, sometimes touching it. At the end of the corridor was a linear-B accelerator. Even now his radiographers were locking the lead-lined doors, ready to throw the switch and watch the screens as the invisible blade entered the patient, still and silent on a metal table. His nurse, Mrs. Leighton, was ready to begin; the rooms were filled, people were waiting. She was 52 today and had white orchids pinned to her uniform. She saw him looking at the flowers, but all she could see was the backs of the petals.

The doctor let her lead the way. She was heavy—no waist—but shapely in the legs and arms. Her face was plain and her eyes lost behind glasses. It was her hair that he liked: bushy and red, cut in a girlish curve. She was from Ireland and when she was in the mood for it, her accented talk and her laughter could fill this office, every buzzing and purring space in it.

He held the stack of charts: Mr. Hockney, Mr. Carnevalli, Miss Thomas, and Mrs. Smith were first. Stapled to the front of each chart was a line drawing of head and body. A circle marked the spot where the malignancy had rooted. Mr. Hockney's circle was on the face, right under the left eye—but there were no eyes on the drawing. The doctor opened the door onto Mr. Hockney and his wife. "Fine and you, Doctor?" the old man said. He had a big head, a liver-colored face with droopy eyes. The wound was on the pouch of the left cheek, a mark that a cigarette might have made. Mr. Hockney liked to joke about it because his wife was a heavy smoker, and the doctor laughed every time. Now Dr. Warren looked into the wound. The skin around it was rosy; the high-energy beam had burned through the cell layers, already active with alien life. Mr. Hockney was not feeling tired?

"No, sir."

"What does your wife say?"

His wife began to say that yes, in the afternoons, an hour or two after the visit, he got a little woozy and went for a nap on the back porch or in the hammock. They talked about hammocks, about the weather and the season so late in getting started. They argued about the right time to unhook a hammock from indoors and rope it around some backyard trees. Mr. Hockney said his wife liked to rush the season. The doc should get himself a nice hammock, he went on, a real canvas job like his, now *that* was living! Dr. Warren got up and asked more questions: appetite, bowel movements, pain? He gave Mr. Hockney a pat on the shoulder of his shapeless tweed jacket. Then the wife wheeled him through the open door and down the corridor.

Dr. Warren saw all his patients, he wrote up some notes, read an article recommended by his nurse, drank a cup of herbal tea, then he called his wife. She wasn't home. The cleaning lady hadn't seen her. And there was no note left about cupboards needing fresh paper or carpets to be vacuumed. Dr. Warren hung up the phone and closed his eyes—when he opened them, there was Rosemary Leighton, with the orchids. The orchids were from him. He bought them on an impulse. He had walked through the hospital lobby on his way to the office—a route he seldom took—and stopped at the florist. He looked at roses, camellias, irises, and daisies, and the girl had arranged assorted bouquets, but he didn't want a bouquet, he said—did she have an orchid? The girl went to the refrigerator and brought out a spray of white orchids on shiny green leaves and tied with white satin ribbon. It was too large, too expensive, but he bought it and carried the square box to his office bathroom, opened it, buzzed the nurse on the intercom, and lifted the flowers from their bed of crushed paper.

It was the busiest part of the day. The office was fully staffed and a new set of patients were beginning to walk or be wheeled to the little private offices for consultation. The doctor was due to make another round of visits. Mrs. Leighton bunched material from the front of her dress to support the heavy flowers. She used the hatpin that came with the corsage and two safety pins the doctor found in his desk. When she was composed, the flush gone from her face and throat, she reminded him that today was Friday.

On Fridays his appointments ended at 12 sharp and he met his staff in the afternoon to discuss that week's patients, many who were here last week and would be back next. Some of them were moving with a painful slowness through their cures: the disease was strong and the therapies ate without discrimination through the cancer and the body. Sometimes the course of improvement would be too slow, or too slow to matter. He remembered arguing with his former nurse that the outcome was mostly good, better than if the patient had only been cut, or cut and treated for pain. The combination—the surgery, radiation, and drugs—was what worked to make a narrow opening that might grow larger. That nurse was unimpressed. The cure was a nightmare, she said, and the disease was a nightmare. But did she know, he said, that only forty years ago, patients with these same cancers simply suffered and then died? They still die, she said, it just takes longer.

He told that nurse that her attitude was unscientific—it was medieval. Why had she become a nurse if she felt this way? She didn't have an answer. She was young then, 22, and her uniforms were all tailor-made out of beautiful imported cotton. She was slim and the dresses, made for her when she graduated from nursing school, were smoothly wrapped around a tiny waist; they had narrow skirts and wide lapels, like uniforms he had seen in newsreels during the war. And she herself was old-fashioned, an only child, who had never spent a single night away from home. He had a new practice then, and not much to pay her. She didn't mind the salary, but she disliked the work and found the cancer patients depressing.

When he asked her what she did for nightlife, she told him about the big family suppers with aunts and grandparents, the homemade beer and wine they drank. She didn't do anything special at night: she read, she watched television and studied. Sometimes she worked in the garden with her father.

He remembered asking her to tell her father that he would be glad to drive her home at night, since her house was on the way home. At first she said no, why bother, her father was retired and had nothing else to do, but he persisted and eventually asked the father, who said he'd be glad not to have to break up his afternoon driving all the way to South County and back.

He drove the nurse, Mary Rainville, straight home for a couple of weeks, then they stopped along the way for drinks, although Mary had never had a real drink besides the homemade brews. She still hated the work, but continued to come to the lab. They were in love.

When they first married, her mother made herself a key to their apartment so that she could keep their refrigerator stocked with homemade dinners; she would also empty the hamper and bring their clothes home to wash and iron. Mary didn't cook or drive a car. They drove to work together until she became pregnant with Anne. She stayed home then, and what did she have to do all day long by herself? She worked in the garden, she said, she talked to her mother on the phone. When the baby arrived, there was plenty to do, but things changed again when her parents moved to a retirement home in Scituate. He had braced himself for a painful break, but it didn't happen right away.

The rain was beating on the window. Every now and then the wind would coil and drive a spray of water against the walls, then die down and the rainfall soften. There *were* patients he couldn't help, and maybe more now that approaches to cancer were so aggressive and experimental. He had a girl so weak she came to the lab in bathrobe and slippers barely able to sit up in the wheelchair. The shrinking of tumors was no longer an important part of keeping her alive, but he had kept her alive. Thin and desiccated, her bald head wrapped in a cotton scarf, she no longer complained of the pain. She didn't have the energy to talk, so her mother talked, but now even the mother came for the therapy silent and rigid. The girl's case was scheduled for discussion that afternoon. He would be candid. What good did it do them to think they were getting well, when there were but a few months or weeks of lassitude and pain with decreasing function? Mary thought they should never be told; that it took hopefulness to live, and if they were that far beyond hope, they knew it already. She was never there at the interview when the family and patient learned of the death day.

Mrs. Leighton tapped on his office door: "It's me." Mr. Belfer had finished painting the men's dressing room; two of the girls had gone to lunch; if it was all right with "the doctor," she was going to lunch; there were no more appointments. Could she bring him something back? He avoided looking at her face. He fixed his eyes on the white blossoms, magnificent on the cheap fabric of the uniform. She handed him a list of patients still in the hospital whose doctors had recommended a course of radiation. Two afternoons a week, he walked across the street to the county general to visit these patients and to prepare them for their cures.

The hospital was not directly across the street. When he walked straight over from his office door, he stood in front of a weedy field with a few shaggy fruit trees and a farmhouse sunk in a ravine. Tied to one of the trees was a Holstein cow who did the farmer's mowing in the course of the summer. With the steady rain, the grass was tall everywhere, even in the spot where the cow stretched his rope to pull the tender grasses with big yellow teeth. Once they saw the farmer and his cow, the patients would ask to move to the farm side of the hospital—and if they couldn't be moved, they would congregate in the sunrooms on that side. None of his patients had the pleasure of this peaceful view. They were confined to rooms facing the power plant: small, cluttered rooms bound tightly around the nurse's station. A gaze from the desk took in half their number; a roll of the chair, and the rest were in view, unless their doors were closed. The nurses were cheery and blank, in perpetual motion around the immobile, the suffering, the stinking, and the feeble. It was a hard contrast, even to him; he had to tell himself that this was only the first step: the tumor might be gone but the disease still raged, and the patients were stricken by both surgery and illness, and soon to have what was left burned and poisoned out of them. Sometimes, even with the supreme effort, the end came quickly, but no one could tell him that the effort wasn't worth it.

He entered one of the rooms, pulled the curtain between two beds, and sat down next to a Mrs. Grayson. (The chart said that Elaine A. Grayson, 55, was scheduled for chest surgery, then canceled; the growth was too large and in an awkward place.) The patient, in a pale blue johnny sprigged with flowers and covered with a thin blanket, was dozing. She had a thin face with fine-grained skin stretched across the bones. The skin was slightly orange. The doctor waited for her to wake up. She *was* awake; she had been watching him through slitted eyes. She saw him study her face and then glance at the arm blackened with bruises from the intravenous needle—"Nail, why don't you call it a nail!" she had said to one of the nurses.

Dr. Warren touched the patient on the shoulder. "I'm awake," she said. "You can't sleep here."

He leaned over the bed to study her head and neck. An incision had been made for a node biopsy and the edges of the plastic bandage were cutting into the soft skin of her throat. He found a small scissors and clipped the sharp points.

"It's supposed to *melt* off," the patient remarked. "And I told them, 'In a pig's eye!'"

Mrs. Grayson had one child, a daughter, living in California. Her husband was dead. He had worked in a button factory until it closed down a decade ago.

Dr. Warren explained that the surgery had been called off for good reasons, and that there was no need for panic; they would try other things; it was hard, but at the very least—.

She smiled at him. A few tears had rolled down her cheeks. "I heard this already," she said. "I got the message."

"Are you scared, Mrs. Grayson?" he asked her. "Don't be scared."

"No one calls me that," she said. "It makes me sound old."

Dr. Warren read the nurse's chart. He noticed a bunch of red roses in a glass vase that was out of the patient's line of sight. "Can you see them from there?" he asked, then moved the vase to the edge of the windowsill. The buds were still tightly closed.

"When the sun comes out," the patient said without looking, "they'll open real nice."

The lesion was discovered only a month ago, and it was well developed, small-cell, the worst kind of lung cancer, although it had not yet spread. He put the chart down and picked up the patient's hand, slick and cold. "Are you warm enough in here, Elaine?"

Her eyes filled up again. "You're embarrassing me," she said. "I haven't even combed my hair today."

"Your hair is fine," he said, "but you haven't told me how you're feeling. How are you feeling today?" A nurse tripped in and answered, "She's feeling much better, aren't you honey?" The nurse went straight to the intravenous sack, checked the needle, and tripped out again. Her stockings made a snapping sound as she walked.

He wrote out the dates of the treatment on a prescription pad. It was painless, he told her, painless and quick. She seemed slightly more interested.

"Is your daughter in town?" he asked, standing and picking up the chart.

"She's coming," the lady said. "And bringing my baby, my granddaughter. Two, not quite two years old she is. And I bet they won't even let me see her."

"When you're feeling up to it," he said. "You'll be out in no time."

But her face had tightened again. She felt around for his hand and held it. "You're young," she said. "I don't know how you can stand it. I couldn't stand it."

We're going to make you better, he wanted to say. It was what he always said.

She looked at his hand, big and freckled. "You don't do the cutting, I can see that." Then she added, "Good thing, huh?"

"Thanks," he said. "You don't like my hands?"

"They're fine. Nice hands." She patted the heavy hand. "I like all my doctors," she said, waving him away. "You're finished here. Go on. You make me tired with all your questions." Her voice sounded a little stronger, less raspy.

"Try to eat something, Elaine," he said. "Tell them to cook you something good."

"*You* tell them!" she shrilled. "You're the one in charge."

He laughed.

Dr. Warren saw Mrs. White, 35, bone; Mrs. Scully, 63, breast; Mr. Ratner, 84, colon. They were all postsurgical, sick, but not as sick as Mrs. Grayson. He was hungry now—and he took the elevator to the doctors' dining room.

No one was in the whitewashed room except old Dr. Caruthers, a county GP, who visited his patients every day in the hospital, even after they had found other doctors. He didn't seem to notice the radiologist coming in. He was having a lively conversation with himself over a fried-egg sandwich and cold drink. At first Dr. Warren thought there was someone else in the room, but no. Many of Dr. Caruthers's patients, he heard, had died prematurely of cancers that went too long undetected. Some said he was worse than having no doctor at all, but his patients— many now deceased—were loyal, never known to complain, and the old doctor was still licensed to operate both here and in the city hospital, although the opportunity never arose for him to pick up the knife with hands that could barely grasp a sandwich: first he picked up the top layer of bread and the egg, then just the bread. Dr. Warren hid his own face behind a newspaper. From across the room he could hear the old duffer cursing and then apologizing.

When he had finished his own lunch (roast beef sandwich, lemonade), and put his teabag in a cup of hot water, Dr. Warren left the table and tried his home number again. Mary herself answered. "I had to go down to the school," she said. "They thought Anne was feverish. But she was all right."

"Did you bring her home?"

"I didn't bring her home. Weren't you the one"—his wife's voice sounded loose and agitated—"who said to let her stay if she wants? She doesn't have a fever anymore. That's what she told me. Unless she's lying."

"I wasn't criticizing you," he said, although if it were he, they both knew, he would have picked the girl up, and left the office full of patients to do it. Anne had had rheumatic fever, so even the slightest illness was a worry. Thirteen now, and a pretty girl, she wanted to be left alone to lead a normal life. The mother and daughter agreed on this point, if about nothing else.

"Oh yes, you were criticizing," she snapped. "You think I don't even know how to take care of my own kid. Well, why don't *you* stay home and take care of her!"

Dr. Warren looked back into the small dining room. Angus Caruthers was still there. Was he listening? "Don't talk so loud," Dr. Warren said. "I can hear you. Why are you so irritable? Or do I know why?"

"Don't you speak to me that way!"

There was a silence. Dr. Warren could hear his wife's uneven breaths.

"Who wouldn't be irritable," she went on, after an awkward pause, "with a sarcastic husband calling home fifty times a day just to snoop!"

He laughed. "Do you call this snooping?"

"I don't care what you call it. Just don't mock me."

He changed the subject. He tried to find things to say that might soothe his wife, stabilize her, but he couldn't find the words that usually came so easily, so he hung up. He called the school and said he would come to pick up Anne Warren, if she was still feverish.

The headmistress sounded relaxed and a little patronizing. She told him that Anne Warren was feeling much better; she was out watching field hockey practice. Mrs. Shanks said she could see her from the window, and she was doing fine. How was Doctor doing? Dr. Warren said he was fine. And Mrs. Warren?

The headmistress wasn't going to mention the fact that Mrs. Warren had been in her office that afternoon, clearly out of her head. It was Mrs. Shanks's way of saying that he should control his wife and let them do their work in peace, but if he couldn't, *she* wasn't going to be the one to mention the unpleasantness.

The waitress was starting to clear away his tea, and he waved her off. Then he called his number again and got the cleaning lady. He asked her to stay in the house until he got home, and where was Mrs. Warren now? Up in the bedroom, she said. And to check on Mrs. Warren, please, from time to time, make her eat some lunch. The cleaning lady liked the doctor; he gave her free advice for her arthritis and for her daughter's migraine headaches. She agreed to stay and help. Call me, he said, if anything comes up.

The tea was cold and it tasted bad in styrofoam. He pushed it away. Somebody was talking. He looked up to see Dr. Caruthers squinting in his direction. At first Dr. Warren tried to ignore him, then he got up and walked to the old man's table. Dr. Caruthers used the time to edge himself out of his chair; he stood, leaning on the table until he was steady. He shook the younger doctor's hand, holding onto the table with his other hand. "Pleased," he said. "Where have I seen you before? I know I've seen you before. Do they call you Terry or Terrence? Right."

"I've heard a lot about you, Doctor," Dr. Warren said, after a minute.

"Sure," the old doctor replied, nodding. "I've heard a lot about you," and he was getting ready to say what he had heard, or at least to think about what it might be, when Dr. Warren said, "But I can't stay."

"Good enough."

"I'm glad to make your acquaintance," he said again.

Dr. Caruthers nodded. He wasn't listening. His right hand was searching the table for a glass with something in it. He shook an empty cup and placed it down with great care. Dr. Warren handed him the water glass, but the old doctor brushed it away. "Where's my orangeade?" he snapped. "I didn't order orangeade today, did I? Grape soda it was. Grape soda it is." He wrapped his fingers around the white cup, swirling a trickle of dark juice packed in ice. "Thank you, sir," he said to Dr. Warren, and gazed at him as he sucked the soda, chewing the ice.

Dr. Warren shook the old man's hand when it was offered, then went and sat down at his own table. It was time to go, but he lingered there. Mrs. Leighton would be waiting to start the meeting—she didn't like to wait. The old doctor had made him think about Elaine Grayson, although it was not negligence that had made her so sick. She was seven years older than Mary, five years older than him, but she seemed much older. It couldn't have been the disease alone that had aged her, but perhaps it had. He had seen youth, or a semblance of youthfulness, restored to his patients once they recovered from the therapies. They never believed that it would happen. It was just at the point when they began to resign themselves to an invalid's life, sluggish and frail, that they felt suddenly fresher, more alert. That was the miracle, but it was the body itself that performed it, once the doctors were through. By then, and he smiled at the irony of it, he was no longer their doctor—they had gone back to their own physician, the one who had told them.

Dr. Warren scraped his chair and the old doctor clucked with annoyance. He had already forgotten their conversation and the sudden noise had startled him. Pretty soon he'd be unwelcome even in the hospital cafeteria. Dr. Warren watched as Dr. Caruthers folded the remains of his egg sandwich in a handkerchief and shoved it into his raincoat pocket. He had been sitting on his raincoat and the back was a mass of wrinkles.

Dr. Warren hurried out of the hospital and across the street. The air was a little drier and wide puddles along the gutter reflected a bluish patch of cloud. The birds were singing in a mild air full of the smell of new grass. He wondered if Caruthers still drove a car.

After the meeting with his staff, Dr. Warren made two calls to consulting oncologists and rang the hospital to inquire about Mrs. Grayson's medication. He made some changes, hoping to give the woman a heavier, more peaceful sleep. By then his radiographers had closed the lab and the receptionists were following them out the door. They were excited. The weather was finally breaking; the news services predicted beach weather for the weekend. He could hear the thrill in their voices as they talked all at once. For a moment he was alone in his small office, barely big enough for his desk. Then Rosemary came in and clung to him. It was not the first time this had happened, and he realized that he, too, had been waiting for what she called a "birthday" kiss, but which, they both knew, was a bit more. She appeared in the doorway, still in her work sweater, carrying the pink jacket she wore home. He had crushed the orchids a little. After helping her into the jacket, he repinned the corsage to its woolly lapel. The flowers drooped. He repinned them. His hands were perfectly steady. He had wanted to be a surgeon and it wasn't at all for lack of dexterity or courage that he'd changed course. The steady hands were resting on his nurse's shoulders, holding her away. He had made the decision to perform only painless cures, the ones that didn't cut into the skin, spread the muscles, or dislocate the inner organs. And now he was locked into a pattern of ordinary days, days spent rotating through his small paired offices, directing the bolt of power to ward off pain and death. This was still his part in the picture.

His nurse said the doctor wasn't paying attention, where was his mind wandering to, what was bothering him that he couldn't tell her? Soon she too left, and he turned off all the lights. When he got out to the parking lot, her gray Chevy was gone until Monday.

Dr. Warren arrived home late. Everything about this day felt different. The cleaning lady had stayed, she had made a strong pot of coffee and his wife had drunk two cups, then showered and changed; she had felt well enough to shop for and prepare an elegant cold supper of shellfish, greens, and fruit salad. She was not in the house when he arrived. The cleaning lady was sitting in the darkened living room watching the news. He walked her out to her car. The sun was bright now and the temperature climbing, but the sky was still thick with clouds. The raw light that cut through these clouds was incandescent when it struck the leaves of bushes beaded with rain. He closed his front door. Light razored into the dark coolness of the house, firing a family picture over the mantle. He walked to where he could see his wife and daughter sitting on the patio, looking out into the garden in its tender early bloom. The plants were trembling with light, light radiant on their faces, too. He stood in the shadow of the house until he found the words to carry him through the bright remainder of the day.

3

Sex-Linked Traits

That winter the latest thing was stovepipe boots. I got them for Christmas and wore them to the college lab, where my teacher said, "Those wouldn't fit *my* legs. They wouldn't even fit over my calves." It was the only thing she ever said to me that wasn't angry or harsh. I was fifteen, fat, but the tall patent-leather boots fit smoothly to my knees. Her boots covered only her ankles, just shy of the balloonlike calves, pure white, in thin nylons with crooked seams.

"Want to try one?" I asked, without thinking.

"No," she said, looking at them lined up under the radiator, with the stovepipes leaning to one side. She waited to see if I had more to say. I tried to keep my face from smiling, twitching, or otherwise showing that I was having a thought. "Why are you standing there?" she demanded. "Do you think I invited you to work with me just so you could stand around and admire yourself?" I started to grin. "There's nothing funny about it. Did you remember to make fresh medium? You didn't. I can see that you didn't."

She took off her own boots and set them near, but not touching, mine. She handed me her tweed coat to hang and the knit hat: a hand-knitted hat, orange, yellow, and blue, with a snowball on the crown. When she wasn't in the lab, she told me, she knitted and her old mother knitted, or sometimes she went to the theater with some neighbors, or played bridge with the Veri-Dames—the Mothers' Club connected with the college—even though she wasn't married and had no children. "And if I did," she once told me, "I wouldn't send them here!" I asked why. "What do you mean, why? Do you have an opinion? I didn't think so. You're not old enough to think for yourself. You may never be." I was tired from a day of school, and my uniform felt tight, although I was empty, not full, and my face was oily from tiredness and not going home to wash it with a drying soap and cooling alcohol. "You should develop your opinions, you know," she said. "You can't start too young. I have no faith in girls who don't trouble themselves to develop their minds. Isn't that what we're put on earth to do?"

When I was twelve I started a science project at school. Every year after that I worked on one and was picked for the state science fair. The students who worked with Dr. Foley in the labs at St. Vincent's College always won the big prizes, sometimes even money prizes. The September I turned fifteen I started going every day to the St. Vincent's labs. On the way over—first I took the bus home from school, then walked the length of College Drive—I stopped at Janet Conneally's house to see if Janet's mother would let her go to the lab. Janet lived in a big white house on a lawn covered with pine trees. In the middle of the lawn was a statue of St. Francis with birds resting on his shoulders and in his hand. Real birds, Janet told me, wouldn't go near him, although they loved the birdbath in the back yard and hundreds came to eat breadcrumbs in the winter and sip the rusty water or peck at the ice. I asked her why and she said that the bluejay who lived in their yard spent his time in the tree next to the statue and bombed it and squawked at it all day long. I thought that was funny, but Janet said her father had to hose the statue down because the jay covered the square pedestal with twigs and leaves and shat on the head and arms. It was a disgusting bird, Janet said, and her brother meant to kill it some night when the next-door neighbors, who could hear and see everything, were asleep. Janet's brother was a freshman at St. V.'s and had made the basketball team, although he hadn't played in a game yet. St. Vincent's was famous for basketball, and it was an honor, Janet had said, just to sit on the bench. Did he know Dr. Foley? I asked. Did he take biology? "Are you kidding!" Janet had screamed. "You've got to be kidding." Janet was a year older than me and attended the high school downtown, where the tuition was a hundred dollars more and the uniform more up-to-date: plaid skirt and white blouse with a navy cardigan. My uniform was one solid color: blue serge skirt and vest, blue jacket, long-sleeved shirt, and blue bow tie.

Janet noticed the boots right away. It was the first week of January and we were back to school. She looked at them, half covered with melting snow and some sand from the roads, and asked me what color the lining was and to fold down the tops so she could see. I told her I couldn't.

"Why?" she asked. "Why can't you fold them down?"

"They're too tight."

I watched her pull on short boots and then struggle into her fur parka. "I don't think they're supposed to be *that* tight," she said.

I didn't say anything.

"They're too expensive for *me*," she said.

I said they were cheap.

She said she didn't mean that. She meant that having the boots required you to have everything else that went with them.

All the way to the lab, as we walked in silence, side by side, I wondered what else the boots might need. And why a girl like Janet Conneally, rich and the daughter of a big shot working for the City of Providence, didn't already have it. That I had nothing to go with them, not even the thought that anything else was necessary, was no surprise to me. I was a reckless person, impulsive—everyone told me this; I was the one who was always going too far.

I asked Janet why her mother had let her come to the lab without an argument, when usually there was a fight and hard words, and once Mrs. Conneally had bolted the kitchen door and stood in front of it. Why does your mother hate Dr. Foley so much? I had asked, and Janet shrugged. It had something to do with being home alone all those dark afternoons with no one to talk to. Mrs. Conneally was forever asking me why "the girl" couldn't stay put just once in a while—stay at home, do something her mother wanted, for a change!

"What does she want you to do?" I asked.

"Sit in the bedroom," Janet said, "while she puts four coats of polish on her nails, then bites it all off."

We laughed. Mrs. Conneally was known for her nerves.

"Go out shopping, make brownies," Janet went on. "Watch the stories."

"Wouldn't you rather?" I asked her.

"I don't know," she said. "Don't ask."

We walked up the hill to the main campus, a circle of concrete buildings with dirt sidewalks and no trees, and turned left into Feeney Hall. We were late because we had circled past the Smith Street Spa for Cokes and to look at Valentine cards. Sometimes the boys from St. V.'s went there to drink coffee or read magazines. Two were there that day, one smoking a cigarette. He pointed it at Janet, or maybe it was at me, and Janet got nervous. She forgot to pay for her Coke, still on the counter, and the druggist ("Hey, girlie!") yelled from his little window. We froze. Janet's face was red under her angora tam. "Jackie," she whispered to me, "feel this," touching my hand with a hand that was cold and wet.

"I know you girls," the druggist said when he got to the doorway. Janet handed him a quarter. The boys—I could see them—were laughing.

"No harm done," the druggist said, taking the coin, but he was wrong. I told Janet, when we were halfway up the hill, that he *owned* the drugstore, and could be as rude as he wanted, but she still planned to tell her father, assistant superintendent of schools, and was sure that the guy's goose was cooked. I wanted to tell her to start fighting her own battles, but I didn't like the druggist, either.

We knocked on the lab door that afternoon, but there was no answer. The door was locked; only the exit sign was lit. Someone told us

Dr. Foley had gone home. When we were late, she often left, and it was—she was always saying—our funeral if the flies starved in the dried-up cake of medium or escaped in the night. Escaped (I liked to elaborate on this when I had my brother Donald as a listener) by collecting in a big army on the underside of the cotton ball that trapped them in their jar. Pushing that cotton with a mighty fly push (I laughed when I told him this story, because he acted it out with a pillow on his head), out they would come. Thousands, millions and jillions of flies, red eyes and white eyes, little flies and big flies would escape into the lab and onto the campus and into the city until they found the bowl of fruit, especially ("Stop!" my brother would squeal when I got to this part) the rotten bananas and stinky apples and split-open grapes they craved. All those days locked up in their jars with nothing to eat but an inch or an inch and a half of smelly agar-agar. My brother didn't know what that was, and I never told him. The story always ended with him trying to hit me and my mother yelling from the foot of the stairs that we were too loud and too silly at a time when we should be settling down to sleep.

Once, dangling off the bed with his hair touching the floor, my brother said, "I think they'd all go to *her* house."

"Whose?" I said.

"*Her*," he said. "Roly-Poly."

"Roly-Poly who?" I asked, because I liked this kind of talk, if it didn't get too babyish.

"Roly-Poly Foley," he said, "the Holy Joe with the big fat ass!"

"That's not funny," I said.

"Yes it is!" he said. "Her house is chock-full of fute fries."

"Say it right!" I yelled.

"Flute flies," he said.

I hit him with my pillow, then whispered, "I heard those flies are coming to hide under your bed tonight—to itch you!"

He was quiet, and I climbed onto my bed, still hot from bounding around.

He said, "Don't tell me that, Jackleen, right before I go to sleep."

"Why?"

"I'll have dreams," he said, in a voice a hair away from crying.

I never had one dream about the flies, but Donald always had dreams about everything. He was babyish and dumb for a ten-year-old—that's what everyone told him—but he wasn't a retard, and he wasn't *that* dumb. Now that I was fifteen, and spent my time up at the lab or on the phone with the cord all stretched out, talking about dates I didn't have to my friend Eileen, who didn't have any either, he hated me the way he hated everyone else, except Nana, our grandmother, who lived with us. She didn't get along with anyone either, and stayed up in her room reading mysteries and listening to her transistor. Sometimes Donald went up there and they played cards or bingo. They were two of a kind, my mother said, when she was mad at them: they were spoiled, selfish, and lazy, Nana and her Deedee. "While *you* spend," she would say to me, "every livelong hour of the day up at the college with that harpy, I'm stuck here alone with them, waiting on them hand and foot, and no one to help me.

"I don't blame you, though," she liked to add. "If I had someplace to go, I'd go, too, and *you*'d have to take care of them." I laughed, and then she laughed.

The white-eyed flies, *Drosophila melanogaster*, were just like the red-eyed ones. Their eyes were white because they had received a recessive trait for eye color from both parents. I was working on a genealogy of the white-eye trait, linked with other traits on the sex chromosome. I kept charts of the series of offspring: f_1 and f_2, f_3 and f_4. The percentage of whites varied with each generation, and my job was to mate the flies: pick a male and female from a generation and isolate them in a jar coated with medium and stoppered with a cotton ball, then wait until pupae were stuck to the walls of the jar. When these pupae had hatched, I would dose all the baby flies with ether and sort them under a low-power microscope. I counted the males and females, the red and white eyes, and then I brushed the flies back into an empty jar so they could wake up. They were not supposed to wake up under the warm light of the micro-scope and toddle off the glass, drop to the floor, and fly away. That would mean I hadn't etherized them enough; the count would be off and the flies would be up on the ceiling, where Dr. Foley could see them. When I watched the flies through the microscope, using the sable brush to roll their little bodies over, I could see everything I needed to see: the tapered male body and rounded female, their different sets of stripes, the eye color, and something that, at first, I didn't understand. I was going to go find Dr. Foley to ask her, but instead I just looked. I looked for so long that some of the flies started to twitch and one tottered around like a drunk on legs like threads. I carefully brushed them all into a jar—it was easy to kill them when they were awake, with their wings and legs stretched out—and no flies were lost, none escaped, and no legs or wings were torn or broken.

I made sure the autoclave was off and all the cotton balls were tight on the jars. I looked into the new jar, with the male and female all alone in there, the white-eyed male and the red-eyed female from the f_4

generation—now they were P5. The male was hanging upside down from the cotton ball and the female was sitting on the lump of agar—was she stuck? I shook the jar and they both buzzed around.

"You love them flies," my brother once said. "Admit it." He was brushing his teeth and I was sitting on the bathtub rim waiting for him to finish so I could brush mine. "You can brush yours," he had said. "There's room. You think I'm poison!"

"I don't love flies," I said.

"Yes, you do," he said. "Just like you loved your rats last year."

"Why don't you shut up," I said. I picked up the *Reader's Digest* that was always there on the radiator cover and looked for a joke I didn't already know.

"Talk to me when I'm talking to you!" he shouted.

He spit his toothpaste out. I was trying to keep from laughing. For my last year's project, I had kept three rats in the cellar and was feeding each one a different diet to show the importance of the four food groups. I had to starve two of them because the experiment wasn't working. "Feed your rats!" my mother was always yelling, just to get a rise out of me. My experiment on the value of a balanced diet proved nothing, but my rats almost became pets, letting me stroke their soft backs when I brought them their jelly lids of leftovers from our dinner. One night, though, the biggest rat—the one I was still feeding to make him look better than the rest—locked his jaw on my hand. Then the lid to the cage crashed down on my finger and broke it. "Sickening things," my mother would say, if the subject came up.

I carried the rats and my chart of their diets to the science fair, but I didn't win anything. It wasn't an interesting project, and all the rats looked healthy, even the two I starved. The newspaper took my picture, though, when a reporter spotted my bandaged hand and saw that I had rats. I got twenty-five dollars from the newspaper, for sacrifice in the cause of science. "Take it," my mother said, even if it wasn't for science but for the sake of faking science that I'd been bitten.

I put the jar of new parents down and went looking for Janet, even though Janet was usually gone by then: she hated the lab and left as soon as she could. Still, I always looked for her at seven-thirty or eight, whenever my work of counting and transferring, making up fresh medium, washing and sterilizing jars, and tidying the lab was finished. I went the long route in case Dr. Foley was still working late with her college student. She didn't like me to go home until she went home, and she didn't go home until nine or nine-thirty, sometimes later. If I waited till then, there wouldn't be time to finish my homework and next day

I'd get in trouble with the nuns, which happened a lot. On my last report card, all my marks had gone down. Some of the nuns did it deliberately: they had met Dr. Foley and they didn't like her. They discouraged any of us who were picked to work with her, but once you were picked, as I tried to explain to Mother Francis Marie, the home-room nun, you didn't have any choice. "Don't be a little silly!" she said, in that automatic way the nuns said everything, but then she said, "Where's your backbone, Jackaleen McManus? And you were the one who was going to show us all."

What do you think I *am* doing? I felt like saying, but that remark was worth a week's detention, and I'd be late for the bus and late for the lab and late getting home for my heated-up dinner and late for my ten-o'clock five-minute call from Eileen, which lasted at least an hour, or until my father went through the roof and started yelling how he'd rip that phone right out of the wall if I didn't hang the damn thing up, and late for bed—with a slap from my mother for not picking up my clothes or hanging up my uniform—and late getting up the next day and late for school, everyone yelling their heads off. All except Dr. Foley, who didn't care how late we stayed at the lab, the later the better.

Winter nights, when Dr. Foley and I walked out on the hard snow of the campus, nobody would be there, and no sound except the stupid pigeons moaning from the top of the gym and Dr. Foley, if she talked at all, which she usually didn't, telling me that if I thought *this* was hard-ship I was living in a dream world. I liked to relax, I was a dawdler, I liked my sleep and my comforts, she told me, and a life in science demanded effort, discipline, sacrifice, patience, good health, mental inde-pendence, indifference to what other people think and to the idle way they live. "Are you listening to me?" she once said, when we had got into the frigid car and slammed our doors.

"Yes," I said.

"No you're not!" she said. "You're thinking about yourself. I was young once."

"I know," I said, trying to be tactful.

"No, you don't know!" she said, driving out of the parking lot—as she always did—like a maniac. My mother used to watch for me on school nights from the upstairs windows, until the time she saw Dr. Foley slam on the brakes after squealing around the corner and going up over the curb so that half the car was parked on the sidewalk. She told me my father would come pick me up after that, on late nights, but nothing doing, Dr. Foley told him when he arrived at the door of the lab: "This girl is not finished yet and I'm not letting her go home and throw a wonderful career in science out the window just so your family can lead a tidy life. Go on back home. You're lucky to have a daughter as smart as Jacqueline!"

I couldn't believe she had talked that way to my father, and neither could my mother when he told her. At first, they just yelled and screamed, then they blamed me for the rotten things Dr. Foley had said. I tried to say something, but they kept interrupting to tell me that never in his entire life had my father been walked on that way. I tried to say she was always like that, and if they thought *this* was bad they should hear what she said to me or to the college student she hated so much. This quieted them down, or at least my mother piped down enough to hear about the college student who was Dr. Foley's special doormat. Marguerite Birch, the girl's name was, and she was studying a sickness called PKU, and, according to Janet, she had it. She wasn't smart enough to be a scientist; she was barely going to finish this year at college and then she was going to be put away to die.

"You're making this up," my mother said. "I don't believe you."

My father had already left the room, after giving me a look that said he was too mad to hear this story now but I would hear from *him* later on.

"It's true," I said. "She's already starting to smell bad."

"What's that got to do with it?" my mother said. My brother had come into the kitchen and sat down at the table.

"Don't you be listening," I said to him.

My mother looked at Donald, then rubbed an orange stain from the corner of his mouth with a little bit of spit on her finger.

"It's a free country," he said.

"Is anybody listening to me?" I yelled, and my mother said, "Finish your story and don't be so bossy."

"She's in the science fair," my brother smirked, "so she knows everything."

I couldn't help but laugh at that, and the tone of it: it was as if my grandmother were in his head talking for him.

"You mind your p's and q's," my mother said.

Then my grandmother walked into the kitchen. She had taken a nap and was still holding her prayer book, which she read to put herself to sleep. "Well," she said, "what's going on here, a little party?"

"No one asked you," I said.

"Don't be fresh," said my mother.

"It's a free country!" Nana and Deedee said together, as Nana sat her bulk in a chair, taking my father's place at the table.

Nana took Deedee's hand after she put her prayer book down. "Shh," she said. "Jack-a-leen is talking."

"Now that you're all talking," I said, "I forget what I was going to say."

"Oh, no, you don't," said my mother. "You're talking about how that girl smelled. *Why* did she smell?"

"What girl?" asked Donald.

"Shut up," I said, and then to my mother, "She's also overweight and has a mustache."

"Who?" my grandmother said.

"Don't interrupt!" I said. "The girl at the lab with PKU."

"What?"

"She's dying of PKU," my mother said. "Whatever *that* is."

I told them (it took half an hour to get it out) about Marguerite and how, in her senior year of high school, she'd won the thousand-dollar award from the medical society for her research on mental retardation—it was the biggest prize at the science fair—and how she used the money to spend a year at St. V.'s. And even though it was all boys, they let her in, the only girl, so she could work with Dr. Foley and attend Dr. Foley's classes. "She makes an extra thousand," I said (although I didn't know exactly what she made, if anything), "working for Dr. Foley as a lab assistant."

"What kind of parents," my mother said, "would let their kid spend every waking hour in a lab with that woman?"

"Her parents are old," I said. "That's why she has PKU. Her parents are too old. They had a genetic flaw."

"How do you know how old they are?" my grandmother asked.

I looked at Donald to see how he was taking this.

"Don't be looking at him," my mother said. "*His* parents weren't too old!"

"I wasn't thinking that," I said, but I was still looking at Donald. "You're the only one," I said to him, "who thinks you're a retard. Nobody else thinks that but you."

Donald told me to shut up.

"Finish your story," my mother said.

"It *is* finished," I said.

My mother looked at me. "Oh, no, it isn't. You were all set to say something else."

I was simply going to say that Dr. Foley treated her much worse than she treated me, but my father came back into the kitchen. He'd been listening the whole time. Now he wanted to know, too. We were all in the kitchen and everyone was gawking at me.

"What does Foley do to her?" my mother asked.

"Yeah," said Donald. "Tell us."

"I can't tell," I said, and a commotion started around me. "She does to her," I said, when I saw the commotion get out of hand—especially since my father was in the room with his belt on—"what she does to me, but worse." They weren't satisfied with this, but they got involved with each other—my grandmother and my father were never in the same room for more than five minutes without finding fault and treating each other to a stream of insults, which usually got my mother involved on my grandmother's side, and Donald, too. Once I said, "It's three against one!" but that didn't make my father any more a friend of mine, so I didn't say anything when chairs began to scrape the floor and ugly tones and tempers flared up.

But I had wondered myself why Dr. Foley was so ugly to Marguerite, when the girl was completely devoted to science—never washed her hair, never bought a new dress, spent her every waking hour in the lab. And she wasn't really retarded, either, just weird. "Two peas in a pod," Janet remarked one day when we were wisecracking. I had to ask her who the other pea was.

"Foley, you stooge!" she said. "Birch and Foley."

I laughed, even though it was mean. "But are they peas," I said, "or flies?" and then Janet laughed.

The night I was mating the *Drosophila* parents, I found Janet on a lab stool writing on a pad. "What are you doing?" I asked. "I mean, what are you doing here so late?"

"I'm doing my homework," she said, "if it's any of your business."

I went over to look at her sheet of Latin declensions. "We did those already," I said, bragging like I always did about how hard my school was, and how far ahead I was, and a year younger.

"Who asked you?" she said. Then, "If you're so smart, why don't you do a couple for me?"

I looked at them—fifth declension—but I didn't do them. I just said them out loud.

"Again," she said. "Slower, so I can copy."

On the way home in the pitch-dark night, my feet freezing in their boots and slipping on the hard crust of snow ("Here, hold on to me," she said), I told her what I had seen. "To do it," I said, "first they back into each other."

"They *what*?"

"They back into each other." But I couldn't really describe it because she had never seen a fly under a microscope and didn't know what their backs looked like or how their rear ends were shaped differently.

"Tell me again," she said.

"They back into each other and stick there, tail to tail."

"Gross," she said.

"They stick there, squeezed together and all puffed out."

"I don't want to hear about it," she said.

"That's all there is," I said. "It lasts a long time."

"What else happens?" she asked. We were only a few feet from her front door, and the porch light was on. I could see into her house where someone was watching TV, and then her mother came to look out the window. She didn't see us: we were standing in the dark.

"I don't know," I said. "Foley calls it a transfer of genetic materials."

Janet looked at me. "You're so naïve," she said.

"Me!"

"Yeah. Plus you're a bullshitter."

I watched her walk up the path and onto the porch. Pretty soon the door would fling open. "Hey, Janet!" I yelled.

"What?" she said, but didn't turn around.

"Flyshitter," I said.

Now she did turn around, and her mother was behind her. I said it in a louder voice, adding, "It isn't a transfer of *shit,* stupid!"

"Jacqueline McManus!" her mother said, then dragged Janet in by the arm and shut the door behind her.

I walked along the sidewalk, carefully shoveled by Mr. Conneally or by Jimmy Conneally, past St. Francis covered in whatever the jay had covered him in that day. It looked like nothing from where I was standing, but I knew you couldn't always see what was there—sometimes the shit was flat and just a gritty streak of green on the white stone. "Stop!" my brother would say, "You're making me sick on my stomach!"

I finally got a grant for my project on flies, "Sex-Linked Traits," and a money prize of three hundred and fifty dollars from the Society of Experimental Geneticists. It happened in June. By the next September, when I went back to the lab, both Janet and Marguerite were gone, Janet to college and Marguerite I didn't know where. At first I thought she was dead, but Dr. Foley mentioned her one day in a fit of rage over a set of pipettes that were laid every which way in a drawer that also contained metal objects. "Did you do this?" she said.

"No."

"Then it must have been Birch. I didn't think it was you."

"Why not?" I asked.

She looked at me—I was sitting on a stool next to hers, handing her one prepared slide after another, which she clamped under the microscope, looked at, made a note about, then discarded, the little glass smashing in the wastebasket. "Are you telling me I'm wrong?" she asked, starting with the quiet voice.

"No," I said, "but—"

"Yes, you are," she said, a little louder, taking a slide from my hand. On it, and embedded in a sandwich of clear gel, was a young moss root exactly one cell wide and growing by doubling its nuclear material, then splitting. It was a perfect act of asexual reproduction and her job was to introduce a shock of ultrasound to the splitting cell to alter it in some unpredictable way. First she had to find a root with an engorged nucleus and puffy cell jacket, the sign that it was ready to divide, then rush it into the inner lab—where I was now allowed to enter, as Marguerite had been, and work, and even eat my lunch on a Saturday—and aim a high-speed sound wave at its silvery skin.

"I never expected you to amount to much," she said, when we had taken a slide to the sound room for Step Two. "You come from an unexceptional background and you've had nothing but those mediocrities as teachers."

I stood in the doorway, watching while she placed the slide in the chamber and directed the beam at it. "You're not a natural scientist— some people are, you know. Your friend Conneally—I forget her first name—*she* was. But all she can think about is boys and clothes. Like you. But you impress me," she went on. "You're either the most reckless person I've ever met or your skin is so thick that nothing ever penetrates. Maybe it's both."

She said more, and not just on that day. I worked for the whole school year and entered an ultrasound project, first in the state and then in the national science fair, in Seattle. I won prizes in both, three thousand dollars in prize money. I called her from Seattle and she said, "Why are you so surprised? Do you think I'd work with a loser?" I also met a boy from a Catholic school in Iowa whose project was on fish, and we went out after the last day of the fair. It was my first date, and I didn't have to ask anybody's permission because my sponsor got the measles and flew home. She left me in the hotel with no instructions. "I don't need to tell you how to behave, Jackie," she said. "You could tell *me*."

When I got back from my date—we went to the movies, then had a Coke in the hotel lobby—I had three messages at the desk, two from my family and one from the principal of my high school. On the bed upstairs was a box of flowers: roses and daisies. "You don't often see that combination," the desk clerk said when I came down looking for a vase. There was a card. I found it later, when I went to throw the box out. "Do you think you'd be in Seattle," it said, "or anywhere, if it weren't for me?"

Before It Blew to Pawtucket

He was hiding in the coat closet, with the boots and the rubbers and among the thin, perfumed scarves, pink or blue, which his Nana wrapped around her neck and under her big winter coat, then stuck a corsage of hard paper flowers and Christmas balls on the collar, and took the long pin with the black bulb—he had seen her—and jabbed it in the back of her hat. Once he asked her why she wasn't scared of this pin, but he'd forgotten what she said. Always it was stuck somewhere under the collar. Now his hand stretched up for it: this was fun (already he forgot the shellacking his father had given him with the belt). Here it was: pearl-sized, and very smooth.

And inside this Nana pocket was a dime—no, bingo marker—and here was a token. Also (he jumped up to pull the light string)—a hankie with a four-leaf clover sewn into the corner. She used to do this kind of sewing: he'd find the packets of thread in her sewing sack, a big flat cloth bag with wood handles. Inside—buttons, thimble, what else? A paper with needles stuck in it, balls of yarn, and these special threads, very smooth and silky, that ladies used to sew into hankies or bureau scarves—he had a scarf on his dresser, blue cloth with a design made from purple, green, and pink threads. It was supposed to be a flower. It looked good, he told Nana, but it was his own mother who'd sewn it before she got married. If you looked close, it was covered with little x's, but if you looked on the back, Nana had said, the back was messy.

A while ago his sister had tried to squeeze herself into the closet but he'd pushed her right out. He didn't want her touching and tickling him. She was a big girl with big feet. She was always talking and sometimes his father knocked her off her chair for talking. Not on the floor flat on her back—it made him laugh to think of that—but just back a ways, and then something always caught the chair after the big arm flung out and cracked across her head. He remembered the sound of it—just thinking of it made him climb inside her coat. "Jesus, Mary, and Joseph!" his father would roar. She didn't know enough *not* to talk! She talked all the time. Him, they couldn't squeeze *two words* out of. "Son," his father would say, "Son, did you hear what your grandmother just asked you? Don't look at *me,* look at *her.* Now *say* what you're supposed to say!"

His sister was just outside the closet door; he could hear her, and he could hear the marble she was rolling along the floor, and heard it when it hit the wall and rolled back to her. Where did she get it? It sounded like a big one, green and glassy. It bumped against the closet door and he scrambled out of the coat, shot out his hand, and tried to snatch it before it reversed. But she had it in her hand already: see? He could see—it was small, but had blue in it; blue was his favorite. She popped it in her mouth, then turned to show him her behind. Then she turned back to let him see her crossed eyes and the marble bulging out her cheek like a gumball. She rubbed her stomach with one hand and patted her head with the other. He could think of things to do to force her to cough up that marble, but he didn't budge. He was kneeling in the closet doorway. He watched the parlor door close behind her, then swing open to show an upside-down head with hair sweeping the floor, then *slam!* He closed the closet door and squirmed into another coat, but now it was too hot.

Silly Billy was walking to school by himself in the light of day, a sickening grin on his stupid face. The grin had been there all morning: he could feel it there. He still had a few baby teeth in the front and they were rotten, very small and wiggly, yellow or brown. Some of his big teeth had come in, but his mother had said they weren't coming in the right way and there wasn't room for all of them. The one in the front was already flapping over the one next to it, so when he grinned, there it was, one covering the other. It looked stupid, his sister told him, and when he stood on the toilet seat to reach the mirror, he could see it and it *was* stupid. These were the teeth that had split his mouth open when he was little. It happened at the beach, while playing on the boardwalk. He slipped (she didn't push him like they thought, but they were already whaling the living daylights out of that brat before he could say so) and rammed the teeth first through his tongue, and second through his lower lip and even the chin was broken up, all gashed and bloody. It was a stinking mess and they had to go straight home and rush him to the accident room. The teeth were sharp then and ragged, but now they were smooth. He used to have a hole in his tongue, but it filled in. He showed her, sticking it way out, and she pushed it back, and said "No, nosireebob."

He was grinning, his face all stretched. He could make himself laugh and keep on laughing when he felt like this, but he wasn't feeling silly now, and there was no one around to goad him. He had run a stick over the links of the Italian lady's fence. Once, when he was little, he had come by to pick the flowers she grew—nice flowers, purple and yellow on tall stems. He picked them for his mother, just the tops. He carried them home in his school hat (BSS, a soft cotton hat with a little visor) and the Italian lady came chasing after him. "What did you *do,* you bad boy! What did you just *do! Give* me those!"

She followed him home, pushing him with shoves on his back. When they got there, she rang his doorbell and then grabbed his hand and held it. "This little boy," she told his mother, "do you know what he just *did?*"

Now he didn't pick flowers anymore, except the ones that grew behind the garage. There was a tall orange flower back there and for a few days he'd watched it and smelled it. It was the only good flower back there— the rest were weeds, that's what his sister had said: hard white flowers, and a few dandelions growing right out of the side of the garage. There were also green flowers, like grass, but with a flowery thing, and some nice smooth ferns. "Those are *ferns,*" she said. "Say it." The orange flower was going to grow all summer, he could tell. Nobody was going to pick it or walk on it. It was taller than the other things, and then one day he picked it—it came right out of the ground with dirt and a big spidery root. He tried to pick out some of the dirt, but there was also a worm and bugs, so he shook the dirt and it got all down the front of him, and by the time he had fixed himself—first by brushing the dirt, then by twirling so the dirt would fly off—the flower had folded up and wasn't any good.

He was going to be seven this month, and his Nana had promised to take him on the bus for a day trip to Boston: swanboats, look in the shop windows, chicken croquettes, public gardens, feed the pigeons. He liked this kind of day, and it would've been just the two of them, no screaming and yelling. (The screaming and yelling was all coming from the girls' schoolyard—he could hear it because he was across the street, walking along the churchyard wall, and now past the rectory wall, up to the corner and stop. He said a prayer for his Nana, Mrs. Mary O'Shea, who had "dropped dead" over the summer. He didn't go to her funeral, but they gave him a card with her name on it. He could read, but he didn't have the card anymore; he lost it, it was somewhere he couldn't find.)

He could hear the children playing and, out of the corner of his eye, he could see the blue pants and white shirts. No children were allowed to play in front of the school and only a couple of girls were there, waiting for the nuns to finish their breakfast, say their prayers, and come waltz-ing and prancing on out their front door, cross the street, two by two, and march up the front steps so that Dorothy Marie Jenkins and Cathy Anne Havens could open the door for them. Good morning, Francis the talking horse, Good af-ter-NOON, Sister Agates and John Bananas. He started laughing and turned his face to the wall so no one could see. He didn't hate the nuns like they said—spit *tooie*—but there wasn't enough spit in his mouth, plus don't spit on the rectory sidewalk or the germy Jesus—no, Jesus's little bird would snitch off your nose. He was laughing more, and sure enough, there was someone at the window, hiding behind the lace curtain to spy on him. (He liked some of them, really.)

He crossed the street on the crosswalk, didn't look either way but nothing hit him, and sat down on the bottom step of the school. These girls would try to get rid of him so they could wait by themselves for the nuns, but he was resting and he wouldn't go. Plus, the second he saw black at the very far end of the convent sidewalk—ba*zoom,* poison gas!—he'd speed to the sidewalks, yikes!

His sister would be in the schoolyard playing with her girlfriends. He had watched: jump over the schoolbags, one-two-three-olara, Callees-up, pies. "Old-Mother-Witch-are-you-ready?" he screamed over his shoulder to the girls. He could see their knees till they hurried to yank their skirts down. "I'M-HANGING-OUT-THE-CLOTHES!" he yelled.

"Shut up," Dorothy Jenkins said, "and get lost." He faced forward, got up, and started walking. "You're weird," he heard one of them say. "He's cuckoo," the other one said.

I'm *weird*, he said to himself, and he liked it. He was nearly in the boys' schoolyard, but he stopped. He always waited, sometimes spinning around and going back down the street to get candy at Jigger's, and sometimes running to stand in the vacant lot behind the girls' schoolyard and look at the girls. Then, at the very last minute, he'd zoom around the fence, up the side, speed across the yard to his patrol line—whoa Nelly!—always late, and everybody looking. Sometimes he was a little bit early and walked into the schoolyard, easy as pie, just as Sister Maglin Joziff ("Magdalen," his sister said, "Joseph: say it") came up, pulled up her baggy sleeve and clanged the bell: dadoom dadoom, da-*doom* da-*doom*. And kept ringing until there were twelve patrol lines and then each one, single file, marched in, girls' door, boys' door, and then they slammed those doors shut, kicked them shut.

He liked to wait, either back here or with those girly girls, even though they hated his guts and laughed in his face. He didn't have any skoo-friends, as his mother called them; no boyfriends, as his Nana called them, no pals (his father). He wasn't palsy-walsy like his sister was. He would watch her, Mrs. Buttinski, in her own schoolyard, big string of gawky gooks following her around, and every morning they came and knocked on the door, knock-knock, who's there? Or, called outside the door: "Ei-lee-een! Ei-*lee*-een!" Once his mother had flung open the bath-room door: he was just standing there looking out the window and screaming back: Eye-*lee-een*!! "*Just* what are you doing?" (She was laughing, so it was okay, except that his pants were down, but his underpants were up, good thing, no one could see.) They came by weekday mornings, Eileen's friends, carrying their books and pockabooks and sat there in the kitchen. His sister would race into the kitchen and back to the bathroom, upstairs and downstairs, until she was told to "SLOW DOWN!" Then she'd sit huffing and puffing at the table, bolt down her food, talking the whole time, jibber-jabber, until the kitchen was filled with girls, then she'd leave, pulling up her socks and having the back of her hair combed and trying ("Ma!") to grab their mother's hand ("You're *hurting* me!") that was yanking at a snarl like a big rat's nest (he was holding his nose and letting the girls see this). Then she'd forget something, or someone would drop a pencil box on the floor and things went rolling under the table and he would go after them and some of those girly girls—"Excuse ME!"—bumping into him. Finally he'd hear them screaming their lungs off all the way down the street. There'd be peace and quiet and his teeth crunched the mixture—Cocoa Puffs and Rice Krispies—that he liked, and his mother burned the toast, cursing and swearing, then there'd be peace and quiet. It was just the two of them and she would read a paperback book or a magazine, so it was really just him. They were the quiet ones, him and her, they never talked, never had anything to say for themselves. When he finished his cereal and part of his milk—and she looked into the glass to see if he finished enough—she wiped his face and his tie, if some dropped there, with the dishcloth and then went back to her book and coffee. He found his schoolbooks somewhere and went out, front door or back door, didn't matter.

He was still waiting but the nuns hadn't come. Now he was in the sideyard, spying from behind the fence. They hadn't come, but it was very quiet. Why was it so quiet? Maybe they *had* come. For a few minutes, he'd been busy. Instead of looking to see if they were coming (two by two, two by two), he'd been trying to poke his hand under the fence to reach a coal on the other side: this was hard and he skinned his wrist, so he covered it with his shirt cuff, then nearly there, touching the coal with his middle finger, when his hat blew off his head, right off his head and against the fence, then kept blowing, so he pulled his hand out—careful—and chased after it before it blew to Pawtucket, and coming back to his place, he noticed how quiet it was, peaceful: where was everybody?

If he moved along the fence, with his back against the fence—step by step, inch by inch—he could see in the basement windows. And there they all were: first grade, Sister Mary Fidelis, with the babies (baby Jesuses) standing at attention, Good morning, Sister Mary Fidelis, Good morning, Children, 8 plus 8 is 16, 8 plus 9 is 27, 8 plus 18 is—. He was talking and someone down there might hear him, so he shut up. He ran to another window—there they were, not doing anything, and the nun not doing anything; it was peaceful. Then all of a sudden, they all ducked down into their desks: he laughed. Out came a reading book, or arithmetic book and soon he heard them all screaming: "Who made you?" "GOD MADE ME!" "Who is God?" "GOD IS THE CRATER OF HEAVEN AND ERT AND *ALL THINGS*."

He snuck from that window to another window. It was the same room and the same children, but now he could see a table with piles of colored clay next to boxes of crayons and jars of poster paints. A sign over the blackboard said: God Is Everywhere.

This was boring but it was also fun. He looked in the next set of windows, but in there (third grade) the boys and girls were facing *him* so they could see him and report him, so he raced right past four windows and stood, out of breath, safe in a space of bricks. It was almost time for the nine o'clock prayer: "O Jesus, through the Immaculate Heart of Mary, I offer you my prayers works joys and sufferings of this day . . ." He knew what prayers, joys, and sufferings were, but what were the "works"? Sometimes he pictured these works as see-through; other times like tinkertoys broken apart, or one thing falling through another thing like a nickel falling down the sewer or through a grate and stranded there. That's what he was, *stranded*. That's what his Nana had said the day they missed the bus back to Providence: "We're stranded, sonny." He was ready to cry but instead Uncle Jimmy drove up from Attleboro, no harm done, and they spent the night with Aunt Jean and Uncle Jimmy, and didn't have to face the music till next morning.

From his place between the windows, he could see the church tower, but no priests could see him from inside the church because the brazier was in the way. Up in the church tower was the little Infant of Prague. He could picture it standing right on the edge, holding its ball, with golden hair and a red cloth on its head, a crown, but a cloth under it, a tiny crucifix on the crown, baby Jesus meek and mild, let me take you for my child, while I sit upon my couch, step on a tack and then say ouch. What color was the blood? He stopped. The janitor, Mr. Mike DiBiasio, was sneaking around on his silent shoes (listen). He was traipsing around with his wire basket picking up trash, or kicking a dried bubblegum with his shoe. The little kids, grade 1, grade 2, were scared of Mr. DiBiasio because he had a stick in his closet: it had a hook on it and a tassel, so if he didn't get you with one, he got you with the other (pain pain puddin'tain)—and sometimes he wore a hankie for a hat, tied in four knots to keep it on.

The nuns didn't go for that (he knew that much) because they didn't like girls putting hankies on their heads in front of the Blessed Sacrament, the BS, but not even Maglin Joziff dared to tell Mr. DiBiasio to remove that hankie.

He was hiding on the side of the brazier, but he could see to where the D.B. was pulling out papers that the girls had stuck, for the fun of it, in the fence-holes. The Dee would be swearing a bloody blue streak and working himself up into a rage. Billy was working himself up, too: he was thinking about how they would take him by the buttons of his uniform shirt and shake, shake, shake until his brains fell out, then take turns slapping him, first on one side, then the other. Take that and *that,* you dirty rat, son of a bee, then they'd pick him up by his shoes, Buster Browns, and bam his head on the ground, or use him as a pogo stick, bam bam, broken skull and broken eyes. ("Don't you lay a hand," Nana would say, "on my Billy boy!") He'd be crying like a baby, boo hoo hoo. Uh oh, there he goes, Mr. D.B., Mister Mike DiBiasio, goodbye and good riddance.

Now he was alone again, but pretty soon they'd come out to get him and drag him into school—he waved to the baby Prague—or maybe they wouldn't. He had feet; he could walk home, one foot in front of the other, until his feet bumped up against the hard penny loafers or black Keds of the truant officer, Mr. Greenjeans, who would scoop him off the sidewalk in a dirty net and off to the dog pound, sirens blaring. He was walking past the rectory and now past the church. He would get the beating of his life and he'd asked for it—or maybe not. Maybe yes and maybe no. He sat down on the church steps for anyone to see and waited for recess, dadoom da-doom. At recesstime, he would go down to Jigger's, buy a rootbeer barrel and take a walk downtown, or to the dump. He knew how to get there. For now, he'd just take it easy, wait for them to come and get him, take a walk on Boardwalk, walk don't run, give him a hot foot and throw him down the sewer. He could see them coming, seventy-six trombones led the hit parade, and he was at the head marching and prancing down Regent Avenue, when a big one came and landed on him, squashed him like a jellyfish.

Eagle Eyes

When she woke, she could hear something and feel something. Was it a bird beating its wings on the roof, and something sticking to the roof of her mouth? He was there, and if she were to ask for something, even while he was asleep with his face to the wall he would hear, and do it. Her hair, tightly curled and bristly, felt like a net around her head, and there was another net of thoughts inside. No one was up—it was late, but no one up—so she could stay where she was, relax. If someone were up, she'd bound out of bed, spring out of bed. He'd feel only the draft, but he'd be up, too; she'd get him up, or he'd get up because she was up. But no one was up.

It would be hot, she could feel the heat through the chilled air blown in from the machine wedged in the window. There was a belt of heat around the bed, and the color of the day was hot, the way it could be hot here, so hot it burned the soles of your feet in their shoes and stockings. You can have it, she told them, the heat.

They *had* had it for five years now—her son, Mikey, and Mikey's wife, Delia. And before that, he had had it the year he came out, and before he met her. Where did they meet? She was going to wake Big Mike up to ask, but she remembered, hiking herself up to see her own face in the mirror over the bureau. It was like his face, mother and son, and she remembered that he had come out here looking for better work—he was a smart boy and educated; they had educated him and he had done his part, working construction summers and in a small tool company after school. He worked, that's how he got where he was, she told her husband. Big Mike listened, like he always did, but he didn't have to be told: he had driven him on his first paper route, when the route was out of town and the boy couldn't get there on foot, and the papers too heavy to put on the bike, remember? She remembered but, she was saying, can't I just say it? They had gotten a few things together for him, and California, it was true, was where the jobs were; you can't find a job around here, she told people. And he found a good job, he still had it, a steady worker, her boy, got up every day and put in a full day, longer if the work was there to do.

There was a wind out there today and it was knocking a branch against the window, so dry-sounding, and the windows clear, yes, but not as clear as you could get them and she had told him: *we*'ll clean them, we'll clean them once and they'll stay that way if he gets on her and she cleans them herself once in a while, say, once a week. We'll get her the ammonia, she told Mike, and everyone has newspaper, that's all you need, and elbow grease. And she knew, she didn't have to be told, that the dust rolled up the street here, and there was a lot of it. Still, if you make up your mind to keep things clean they stay clean, and it wasn't as if the girl hadn't tried, she was all right, likable, but the quiet type, there was almost nothing to her, nothing on the ball.

It was at a party, she remembered; they happened to join the same church and it was some get-together—or was it at a lounge? She shook Big Mike's shoulder, still big and strong, although how old would he be this May? 60, must be 60, 59 or 60, but before he could answer, she remembered what Mikey had said: St. Patrick's Day, and the girl, Delia, Irish descent. They met, fell in love, got married (June first, 1978—there was a picture on the TV of the whole wedding party, bridesmaids, ushers, the girls' folks, and them, she had her arm looped through Mikey's), and had a baby. Everything had happened, she was telling Big Mike just last night, for the best. It was not important that he'd married that other one—Lucy? Laurie?—a troublemaker, and so quick to spend a dollar; he hadn't found the right girl. People make that mistake nowadays—.

Was somebody up? She threw her legs over the side, and so fast her heart was beating the way it could, too quick and uneven. "Mike," she croaked, but couldn't make her voice reach him, so tried again. He was awake now and hovering over her, but she was better, the worst was past. She was turning her head to tell him for the sixth or seventh time— was he deaf?—to stop worrying, she was fine, when she saw the door open, and there was mother and baby. Before he could stop her, she was on her feet. "Your mother-in-law here—" he was trying to tell Delia, but she talked over him: "Baby's sleeping, you with the big mouth!" He knew, didn't he, not to scare the girl or the milk'd go bad and yet here he was, first thing in the morning—. The girl said she had just fed Baby and thought Grandma might like to see little Jessie all fixed up for the day, a big smile for Grandma, see? The baby was asleep and here *he* was, with no shirt on. "Go put your shirt on," she said, "in front of ladies." The baby had milk on its cheek and was that a scratch or a little pimple?

It wasn't hot—12 noon and she'd already put some pastries in the oven, half of them meat, half fruit—it was roasting, steaming! Big Mike was looking out the window at the heat; the only real window was a sliding door that gave onto a patio, all closed in with a high wooden fence. So, what could you see, even if you burnt your eyes gaping in the glare? Nothing. A dry wood fence all faded in the sun ("They're *made* to look that way," Little Mike had said), and a hose hung on it. But it was a drought they were having ("How can you tell?" Big Mike had asked, and hadn't meant it sarcastic, it was just a question), and no need of a hose because it was against the law to water—imagine! There was a lawn chair out there and a birdbath surrounded by painted stones, a few tomato plants were staked to the fence, and a flower garden with nothing in it but "ground cover," as they called it. She had touched it, very stiff, and the flowers opened in the morning and closed at night. (Here they are, she had told him the first trip out, in beautiful sunny California, with everything to see and no windows to see it. Or even if they *had* windows, all these walls blocking the view. "What view?" he had asked. A big parking lot, gleaming with new cars. There were no old cars out here, he observed, when Mikey drove them in from the airport, and they spotted their first palm tree and saw the Mexican names for everything. You have your ocean and your mountains, Mikey had said. A drive of half a day to a day and you're in Vegas or Gold Rush country, twenty minutes to Disneyland, less to Knott's Berry Farm, even less to Capistrano, and a little over a ten-minute drive to the beaches, beautiful sand beaches.) But it was winter now, and no one went to the beach in winter, even though it was just as hot as summer, hotter.

He was still looking. He had his green nylon shirt on, black pants, and sneakers. He had never worn sneakers before, even though Cleveland ("I kid you not," as he would say, and now she said it) can get hot of a summer, but that first trip out Mikey had driven him to the mall and bought him sneakers so they could sightsee and his feet wouldn't hurt him. And so he wouldn't be up half the night, she added, cutting his corns and bunions. She had never seen a man with such bad feet, but he had always had them, ever since she'd known him. It was from standing all those years in the Ford plant. Anybody's feet, she told him, would've given out, and long before yours. He loved the sneakers, white with black trim, and the name brand on the back; he wore them all the time now. "You'd wear them to bed if you could," she said, "admit it."

He had them on now, even though, with a new baby, there were no plans for an outing; enough to do at home to keep them all busy and out of each other's hair, but already—it was only lunchtime and they had eaten—he was doing nothing. She was ready to speak up: there was work to do for those willing to do it, and they were both good workers, when she heard Delia and Mikey in the kitchen. They had stepped out to see a neighbor. ("How do you know your neighbors with these walls?" she had asked, "and no clotheslines to meet over, no grocery stores, just a parking lot, and everybody drives?" Delia had said that people here were very neighborly and lots of young children. Oh yes, she could see this, because the girl was in and out all the livelong day, "but where do these children play?" There were no lots, Delia said, it's true, but there were better places to play.) When it came to California, Delia could be sharp. She was always defending it and there was nothing to defend—it was a beautiful place and the work was here, any fool could see. But it was different, things were done different, and some of the things that were done—. But, she told Delia, live and let live was Mike's philosophy, and now it was hers too.

He had been standing at the window a long time. "What are you gawking at?" she asked. "Nothing," he said. But you can't stare at nothing for hours on end. She was holding baby Jessie, and had been holding her since she woke up from her nap at quarter to ten. She held her through lunch, only giving her back to her mother at the regular feeding time. "This," she told him, sitting there with the little baby in the crook of her arm and her large hand around the baby's middle, "you could get used to, it takes no getting used to at all." But then Delia came to fetch the baby for a feeding. When they were safely out of earshot, she said to him, "If the mother would only use the bottle once in a while, *I* could feed Jessie and they could run out day and night, if they want to. I'd be here to mind Jessie." Mike said this might amount to what they called interference, but she said it was just a thought. She didn't announce it like he thought she would, when the subject of the feeding came up. She started to bring it up—and the tension was there before she even said a word. How did they know what she had to say?

That day they packed up the baby, and took mother and dad in the car to the beach, although it was 120 degrees in the shade and no shade at all on those long boring beaches. Little Mike was at the wheel, Big Mike in the back with Delia, and *she* held the baby in the front, next to her son. They were catering to her, she knew it, because she didn't want to leave the air-conditioned house—dark, yes, but she didn't mind the dark, it made you think cool. She and Jessie could have spent the time sitting and watching the TV, or listening to a radio broadcast, if they *get* radio out here. "We get radio, Ma," said little Mikey, in that tone no one liked. Anyone could see that they were getting on each other's nerves.

It had started a couple of nights ago, and she could feel it building. Two women "fighting over the pots and pans," as Mike put it, never works. She was willing to take over the girl's kitchen, give her a break, give her the time to feed the baby and time for herself, if she wanted it.

First, she had had Big Mike drive her out to the market, where she had spent her own money—$122.40—things were not cheap here. She had kept an account of every expense for all their trips, which they now took by car, cheaper, and you see more—although what did they see but freeway and more freeway, and exhausting the trip was! But still, a moneysaver. After a few of these car trips out and back, she had covered the Rand McNally book with small notes, and filled another spiral pad with details about reststops, coffee shops, motels, sightseeing, toll booths, even the hospital in Salt Lake City, Utah, where Mike spent a night and day with heat exhaustion. She was cooped up in a Howard Johnson's—too high!—but the only room available close enough to walk, and not that close.

She had made a short list on the back of the church bulletin, but then went out and bought five sacks of groceries, everything she'd need for baking and a few suppers, some good-looking cuts of meat, plus some of the extras Delia always seemed to be cutting back on, and set to work, first putting the groceries away, then rearranging things in Delia's skimpy pantry: a single row of canned vegetables and baked beans, a package of food coloring, birthday candles, and cake-decorating tubes.

Of course, the girl wouldn't go for this, and Mike told her she went too far, but she'd do it just this once, get the kitchen stocked and organized— no big deal, no one would even notice, forgive and forget. She cooked Little and Big Mike's favorite that night, a goulash from an old recipe she was always trying to give Delia, but the minute she put pen to paper, she forgot half the ingredients. The children were gone for the day; Little Mike was at work and Delia had driven forty miles with the baby—too far!—to visit a sister. By the time the girl got back, and then him, every-thing was ready, plus bread made, a few extra dozen cookies and fruit squares—a new recipe—baked and cooling, the kitchen spanking clean, and the upstairs and the downstairs bathrooms scrubbed. He had fixed all the dripping faucets and the broken towel rack, watered the flowers— that was a mistake, but he didn't know any better, no one had told him— and simonized the car left at home, the good one, a Mercury, blue with blue trim. All this, and they had fixed themselves up and were waiting, all smiles, for the little bundle.

It didn't go over. You could tell the minute she walked in, sniffing. He liked it, you could see he did, but changed his tune to suit hers. "What else can he do?" Mike had said. "He has to live with her." Little Mike took them aside that night and said—she'd never forget it—"Delia likes to have the kitchen to herself. You're the guest, Ma. You've cooked all your life, you're always saying. Now you need a break. Well, take it, Ma. We'd like you to." He was being tactful, where the girl might not have been, so it blew over. They had a nice dinner—which is all she'd ever wanted to do—give them something nice and let *her* relax with the baby. So, by the end of dinner, when she was up and clearing plates, they told her again, and in a sharp tone: "Sit down!" but she helped and it all got done very quickly and everyone could relax and watch a program, and they did—although, as they sat in the living room with the blue fog of the TV falling on the rug, there was something in the air she didn't like. First, the room was dark, no lights—"feels like a barroom," she said, especially with Mike smoking. He was keyed up and chain-smoking those old Camels, enough to make your stomach turn, but she didn't want to start in on him. Poor Mike, he had to listen to them all and all their gripes, and never a peep out of him.

But that was then and now was now, and they were nearly there, everyone thrilled to catch sight of the ocean, so blue under the blue sky, just seeing it made you cooler, sunny California, she was saying, is really sunny California, no one was kidding no one. There were birds up there, seagulls, but otherwise all clear blue sky. They don't have a blue like that in Cleveland, she thought, although the sky is blue in winter, pale blue. "It can be pretty," she said out loud, "if you give it a chance." Little Mike walked around front to open her door. Her skirt was hitched up tight around her legs. "I'm stuck," she said. He offered to take the baby, but nothing doing, she would manage. Big Mike and Delia then rushed ahead to stake the umbrella and set up a chair for mother. She could barely see them. "Why do they have to go so far?" she said. "All this room, I could sit right in front of the auto."

Over the hot sand, so smooth and white, rippled from the wind, she trudged, clutching the baby, with Little Mike holding her arm. She had rubber-soled oxfords on, and felt secure on her feet. It was only the nervousness of having the little charge, so precious, that made her shaky. It was a very long walk and the heat of that awful sun beating on her head with the frizzy permanent—"a mistake," she told Mikey, especially since no hat in the house, not even his, fit over it—and drops of sweat had gathered and were streaming into her eyes. Her dress was sopping. If only she could breathe, it'd be fine, but who could breathe in this heat? Mike kept his baby shielded with a towel—which didn't make walking any easier. She could barely lift her feet with the weight of the baby and the hovering father. But they got there, finally, and the other two flew at her—took the baby—asking a million questions. It was a wonder she didn't fall flat on her face and have the heat stroke right then and there.

When they had settled her in the chair, and replaced the little bundle on her lap—tears were in her eyes, so what could they do but give back the sleeping baby?—she breathed again, sighed, the tears pooling at the corners of her mouth. Through this she was smiling, but no one saw. They were gazing at the water, so she was free to hug the bundle in peace, her face hot and red, fresh tears rolling down her neck and into the front of her dress. "All right now," she crooned against the roar of the ocean. "All right now," soothing herself until, after a fresh flood and swallowing the sticky ball in her throat, she *was* all right—she could breathe. The hard thing was hiding it from them, and hiding the pain, or else this baby would be whisked right out of her arms, the poor sweet thing fast asleep, even though the big heart thumping against it, plus soaking wet and burning hot. No one knew this, and thank God.

A big green wave was coming in, then another. The waves here, when you could finally see them (and for a while she could see nothing but a swarm of colors) ran, in a perfectly straight line, from one end of the beach—the longest beach she had ever seen—to the other. They came one after another evenly spaced, and right before the shoreline, tipped over and spilled, spreading a sparkling foam over the dark sand. It was then she saw the thing that, no matter how many times they explained it, she'd never believe her eyes—plus this wasn't the first trip to the beach, so why hadn't she seen it before? But she hadn't. What she was seeing was this, because there was no way to be sure but to watch it again and say. This is what she saw:

A person out in the deep water, way out behind those thin lines of waves, had hauled in a plank or two-by-four (she couldn't quite see what it was, but it looked smooth). And there was another man with his own plank. They were resting it—it was more like a float than a raft—on the water. The first one bellied up on his plank—so far, so good—and paddled in until the line of waves was behind him. (Someone took the baby out of her arms and adjusted the umbrella so the coolness fell right on her face.) Suddenly the line sharpened and rose, and the man, flopped on the plank, was lifted. And then—she couldn't believe this, but was cheering; they could all hear her cheering and they laughed, she sounded so happy— he got up and stood on the plank—if he wasn't standing on the water itself!—and was slammed and zoomed into the shore, right on the smooth back of the wave, then right in the cup of it. Then he toppled, and the plank spun in the air like a stick. She could see it now, it had a fin, it wasn't just a piece of lumber. It spun up, twirled, and dove back into the water, crashing, because the wave had gone. You could see the man's head as he washed up in the foam. She was standing and cheering because, never in her life, nowhere she had been, and nothing she had seen—and she had lived through plenty!—was like this. It happened again. "Ma, they do it all the time," Mikey was explaining.

She looked up to see how *he* was taking it, sitting on the sand, his legs sticking straight out. Did he like it? The second time wasn't the same. She let out, on the third one, a squeal that made them all laugh, but it wasn't funny. She settled back in her chair, a chaise lounge—she slumped in it, closed her eyes: it was black there. When she opened her eyes, all watery in the light, Mike was still there beside her, right out in the sun and the heat. She reached out her hand but he didn't take it. She had to clutch his arm, pinch it, till at last he opened his big hand for hers. She tried to swing his arm with hers, but his was rigid. She tugged at it again, and tugged until the big arms finally swung together, back and forth, over the baking sand.

The Calling

The call came on a winter afternoon. Was it the day she found the ten-dollar bill in the hallway? Together they earned about fifty a week, enough to buy groceries and pay rent on the apartment above the dentist's office. That ten could take them to the movies, or buy a cheap but lavish lunch at the English Tearoom. They'd been married one month. He had taken their wedding presents—a blender, portable oven, electric broom, and frying pan—and sold them (brand new, half-price) to the dentist and his assistant. Then he bought himself his first sound system. They might have, he said, no wheels, no cash, and live in a one-room hovel, but now they owned a turntable, and pristine speakers, and a powerful receiver.

She didn't miss the presents. What would a couple of paupers—without so much as a carrot or a bag of beans left over from one week to the next—do with a twelve-button blender or an electric broom (their plank floor so warped and splintery, you had to wear shoes to walk to the bathroom)? They had married very suddenly. They were castaways ("bums," her family thought; "beatniks," his). Both families still had children at home to guide toward decent lives. *They* had decided to be artists. Everything else would come second. Marriage would furnish a twin soul for the hard life, stabilize the household with a good dose of reality: the need for shelter, food for two mouths (not to mention costly art supplies).

It was agreed that one would work, but when neither wanted to sacrifice everything to the other, the plan was modified. They'd each contribute fifteen or twenty hours a week to upkeep—he clerked in a bank; she babysat; she waited on tables; he mowed lawns; they both cleaned houses; he was a stockboy and "lifted" the occasional leather jacket to sell to the dentist. Thus they scraped by week to week, sometimes saving enough for wine or some smoke to offer his artist friends—for as long as they kept coming. At first she didn't know why they'd stopped. He'd asked them to, he said: it was the first rule of a productive life. What was? That you were married *or* you had friends, not both.

That day they had chosen lunch. The ten-dollar find, supplemented with
a few singles, was enough for the main course *and* dessert. The low,
narrow restaurant was hot and clattery; they had to wait an hour to
claim a table near the bay window, steamed and now frosted in wide
swirls. She studied the ice veins scribbled over the frost. Soon savory beef
dishes, bedded on rice, were brought with glasses of red wine, an extra.

He was brooding. He wouldn't say about what. He was sorry if his
mood—he was just thinking, working in his head—cast a pall on her
outing.

Cars wheeled by, their headlights flowered in the opaque glass, while
slower-moving bodies, walkers, shadowed the table's white cloth. "How
about you?" he asked.

"I'm fine," she replied, swirling the ice cream pooled on the hot Indian
pudding.

"You want to eat," he quipped, "but you don't want to work."

She smiled. It was only three, but the day so overcast, lamps were burning inside and out. He lifted his glass and swallowed the last of the wine.

They walked home through a steady snowfall. The sidewalk was cribbled
with ice from an earlier storm, a quick thaw and freezing rain, but the
street was wet, crackling with salt the trucks had just dumped. She stared
into darkened shop windows, their glass floury with drifting snow.

He was holding her mittened hand, smoking with his free hand. It
seemed life could go on like this forever—wintry, lonesome, the two of
them bonded together in poverty, by vocation, in their (as he put it)
"socially parasitic" union. Now that she had the time, she couldn't settle
on a project. With an old-fashioned, leather-wrapped Rollei, gift from his
father, she had set out every morning in search of pictures like those shot
early in the century—the sheets of raw terrain, splintery, sun-drenched
shacks, aerial shots of hats or umbrellas forming rings or swirls, the many
galleries of human freaks. But the shooting impulse was no longer young,
and the world altered by tens of thousands of one-of-a-kind pictures.

With the camera slung around her neck, she tried to feel bold. She
stalked, tireless and aggressive, but you didn't just stumble on the jarring
coincidence, the scene suddenly flushed with meaning. Those richnesses
were seldom glimpsed, even by those without a camera. You needed to be
a kind of rarity yourself, she figured, to draw the really rare things.

The few dozen prints she'd made each contained, she told him, less
than any good snapshot. His advice was to "shoot people you know. Your
family, for instance. That's what you like about snapshots," he added.
"Discover the unfamiliar in the domestic. Play with it."

People had seen enough of themselves in photos, she told him.

"Not the people *you* know. Their problem is," he said, "they've *never* seen themselves."

Since he'd always inclined toward abstraction, his paintings were, as he put it, "radically depopulated." He exulted in his solitude, in his material: rolls of canvas, heaps of drawing paper, rags, brushes, paint tubes, and quarts of vaporous solvents. For a year now he'd filled square upon square of primed and unprimed canvas. (Luckily, the dentist had made space for them in his basement, where he stored old dental chairs and cabinets, antiquated drills fanned with metal trays.) At first he spent hours down in storage, studying finished work under the naked light-bulbs, shuffling and restacking it. He borrowed her camera to catalogue his work on slides. Then suddenly he changed course: what he needed was a three- to five-year work zone of uninterrupted application. Later on he could sift through the trials, the series, sort and judge. First, he needed to strike: there was untapped force in him. He worked long days in the one-room apartment, lining the walls with wet canvases; then he stripped the walls, crated up the paintings, and started over. His progress was rapid—there were already fifteen numbered series—with never a slowdown or respite long enough for even a moment of self-doubt. He worked in a mental space cleared every morning by a session with his barbells and a red-hot shower. He took only the occasional Sunday off and, if they had the cash, they went out.

They had been home that night only fifteen minutes—lamps were lit, wet clothes removed, Oscar Peterson "Live at Montreux" spinning on the turntable—when the phone rang. It took him a long time to find it, buried in the closet.

Did she hear it first from him, or was it only when she'd grabbed the damp receiver and heard her aunt's croak? The voice was swamped. "Speak up!" she said, but the aunt broke down. Someone else, a neighbor, picked up the phone. By then, *he* must have spoken, hovering behind her, walking away, then back again. The neighbor was talkative, but at that moment she didn't want to hear the details. Her brother, Franko, was dead. She was anxious to hang up, but once the connection was cut, she picked up the receiver and dialed home. The line was busy.

It was then—before the landslide; no: quicker, a fusillade; napalm, she told her sister, who said it was more like slow electrocution—that she saw that he was holding himself back. Later he would say that this—the capacity to transcend the personal—was art's gift, but even then she knew it wasn't art that was helping. His face—when visible, for he kept his head down—was flushed, the jaw clenched. The sense came faster to him, she figured, and he tried to fight it.

Watching him (she thought of the astronauts' faces shot while suffering unbearable gravities), she felt herself sheltering in the cold box of the room. He made her a cup of tea, passed it with a shaky hand, but when she refused to answer even a single question, he left the house.

Dusk had come early. It had begun while they were sitting in the tearoom, but still it lingered. Their tall windows, facing an alley, were cross-hatched by bare branches sleeved in ice. A heavy cloud bed had sunk to the level of the treetops. The white night was windless. Inside— she had turned off all the lamps—it darkened first, the air thickening in the corners. Then the thin branches lost their sharpness and soon, clouds, trees, and cement-block garages were webbed in a dense screen.

Franko, the only boy, was three years younger. As children they were close, sharing a small bedroom and Saturday-night tub. The bathroom was right off the kitchen and knee to knee they soaked while their mother, a few feet away, washed the supper dishes. Sometimes shrieking "This Old Man," or "Old Mother Witch," until she pounded on the flimsy door for both of them to shut the hell up. She didn't hate them, but now that there was a third, raucous baby, the Porky Pigs, as they called themselves, giddy and shrill, could push her right to the limit. *He* could be set off, she knew, by the smallest thing: a pantomime of how and where the worms came out, herself as hula girl in Kleenex costume, or simply the sight of two fat toes ambling up the wall of the bathtub only to be—timber!—clocked by a Frankfoot.

Sometimes while she soaked, he, naked or in footed pjs, perched on the toilet thumping the strings of his green guitar while she blew into a Coke bottle, or rubbed the squeaky sides of the tub. They sang, high voices fluting over the full tub, its water tepid and greasy from all the junk plopped into it. He would wheel in the red wagon piled high, and they drove his metal trucks, somersaulted her naked dolls, bounced soft rubbery balls and small jacks' balls, dunked his bright-colored cowboys and soldiers, horses and rubber Indians and some rusty boats. When he stepped in, the booty—the stuff that floated—would surge and bump against her belly and arms, then she'd sweep it all back. On the hard bottom was a painful garden of jacks, gumball prizes, tinkertoys, and marbles—whatever happened to be in the wagon. If she'd told him once, she'd told him at least a thousand times, Don't do it! But he always pitched in everything—broken, rusty, even stuffed.

They were allowed half an hour to soak because they were "grubby!" "foul!" "filthy as a couple of coalmen!" This caught their ear and next they planned an assault on the coal slide—first, wait until the coalman opened the bulkhead, then distract him (one of them, say, scream bloody murder), while the other made a dash for it. In the end, all they got was a view of the hole as the coals thundered down the ashy slide and hurled to the cellar floor. It was pitch dark down there.

From then on people kept splitting them up: first it was no bath together, then no to a shared bedroom. They rarely had time to tune their moods, or—through some dumb joke, the bad names they had for everyone, the sickening words for food—ease into a routine. She went to school all the livelong day; he stayed home, sulked, pinched the baby, or drove in Daddy's car to the market.

The next year, he went to school, too, but came right home again—too babyish. The nuns said wait a year, what's the rush, so by the time he started first, she was already in fourth, a big girl, know-it-all, she played the girly games: leap-over-the-schoolbags tag, pies, Red Rover. He watched through the fence that cut the schoolyard, boys from girls. There he stood, next to the brazier, peering through the links at clumps and strings of girls in blue jumpers. "Hey, Stupe!" he would call. "Queen For A Day, Mrs. Cornflakes!" She heard, but never answered, never called his name through the schoolyard pigsty—"St. Pinks," he called it, although the name was St. Philomena.

"I saw you," she'd insist when he came home crying to Ma. "I just didn't have time to look you up." She would say things like that, big pocketbook and earrings. He liked it. The whole family said she treated him just like a bum—like dirt under her feet. "Yeah!" he agreed, happy for once to be the center of confusion. Then, she'd make sure he saw her raise her shoe to show exactly the kind of dirt he was.

His trouble started later on. By then, there were four of them—the extra one came when he was in second grade, and the crybaby in first with St. Pinks' witchiest teacher, who shrieked at the children, tore from her desk like a shot after some dopey boy with gum stuck to his hair, and beat, beat, beat! The poor crybaby—they called her Mayday once a new crybaby arrived—was scared out of her wits. She was a dumbbell just like him, and full of backtalk—not like *her*, perfect, go to the head of the class. "Go to the Head of the Class," a game he loved, although, just like Mayday, he hated school. So that year when Mayday was on the hot seat every day, and their father was out of work half a year, and Ma caught two kinds of pneumonia, he "got started," as they said, but no one noticed right away—they had other fish to fry.

Loaded down with books she'd lugged home—sometimes took the bus, sometimes hoofed the whole two miles from St. Pink's High, sweaty, tired (he swore he could see the moods on her face)—she would race to the bedroom, slam the door behind her. St. Pinks Grammar was out at three, so every day he dawdled because no one was home except Mayday and Babyanna—Chickenbaby, as they called it—asleep in its crib, or screeching, Mayday slinking away. Mayday hung over the Chickbabe's crib: ugly faces, tease, pinch, and, once, had hauled the heavy, smelly baby to Ma, a hand clapped over the CB's mouth tight with howls, then dropped it right on the linoleum, and was given a good clout. So Mayday learned to plan her attacks for moments when (Ma hanging clothes, or on the avenue) the CB could yell its damn head off—with the help of a blanket flung over its head—and no one to hear.

This was all he had to come home to, so he waited for the high school girl. Sometimes opened her closet full of big clothes and dusty shoes; sometimes looked under the bed to see what she had hiding there. One fine day she caught him. Flung open the door, booted that rear and his head clunked the bedframe. "Hey!" she said, "Nothing under there for pigmeat," then pushed him out the door. He leaned up against it, begging, and Mayday there, too, curious, finished with the CB for that day, or maybe the CB wasn't home.

She was too busy for him: homework, phone calls, and primping every night at the bathroom mirror. He had nothing going for him, as he said, in his life. Someone found him a pack of Boy Scouts, and then he memorized the responses for serving daily mass—took him months—then, go to the head of the class. He smartened up just about the time he was knocked flat on his back, fainted in the schoolyard. One of the nuns, or maybe the janitor, hauled him up to the principal's office. When it happened again—right before Sunday dinner—they rushed him to the hospital. "Can I come, please, pretty please?" she begged, but no. It was his trip, his funeral. When he came home, her door was bolted. "Hey," he yelled, through the keyhole, "I'm back." No answer. At supper that night she saw his face all mustardy or maybe they were eating hot dogs that night. First it was mustardy, then mayonnaise. "You look like egg salad," she said, and he, who laughed at everything, laughed, but "Mind your own beezix, Chunky," he said after.

"Skin Milk," Mayday called him, or Mr. Instant-Potato-Head, and he couldn't help but laugh at that. But with the long face came the ugly moods. He was sharing a room with his Daddy, twin beds for a pair of crabs. Mayday slept with Ma and the Chicken, and the big girl had her own room, "Keep Out Bums," still pinned to the door. But Ma felt crowded, so the Chicken was out. Big girl had her choice: CB or Mayday, but "nosiree," she said, "I pick poison," meaning him, but he wasn't budging, boys with boys, said Ma, but there were other reasons.

If she stayed up late ("She's readin'!" Mayday would hiss, if so much as a stick of light rolled out onto the hallway carpet), and waited in the dark, she heard. Groans, coughs, up and down to the bathroom, poop and fart, and sometimes throwing up. She was asleep again before the commotion was over. No wonder he always looked so tired. "Your face looks like snot," she said, but no rise from Sonny, no son rise.

It wasn't her fault, she whined. "Don't be such a little goon!" her mother said. Still, how had it happened? They could hardly squeeze a word out of him. His disposition, Ma said, was sour as an old man's, and he was young! Luckily, he had a few playmates, who stuck to him thick and thin. He picked his chums from among the holy joes, boys with "a calling," so he decided—what else?—that he too could hear the calling. And then it was nothing but church, rectory, visits to the Blessed Sacrament, rosary, novena, and daily mass. At home it was nothing but whine, sulk, cough, puke, and bellyache.

"What in bejesus is wrong with you, Franks?" she demanded, ticked about the chip that nothing—no word, no look, no foolishness of hers—could knock off.

"Dry up and float away," he said, which overhearing, Ma yelled, "Don't make him commit a sin!"

"What's *wrong* with him?" she asked her mother. "Don't tell!" she heard behind her, wheeled around and there was Franker: a beefsteak, lobster, a hotball. "What the heeber's wrong with you?" she yelled in his face. She didn't want to make him cry, or even to get the punch she got—and hard—for being a nosebag.

Later Ma took her aside: "He's got ulcers. Now are you satisfied?" But she knew that wasn't all.

"Don't you have any sense?" Ma was still talking. "Don't you have feelings?"

In high school, they operated. First, they thought they'd gotten them all; the second time, they weren't so sure. They cut out what they could and sewed up what was left—not much, a belly the size of a Bolo ball. He picked at his measly snacks morning and afternoon, thin as a rail, and moody. But slowly—over a year, or two at most—he got better. Looked the same, but more outgoing, "out of his shell," Ma said, and next thing, bolted the seminary and back to high school; then it was nothing but hockey and basketball, guitar, "juice" and juice babies. She came home one summer from college and banana-yellow he was, fizzy as beer. This, she reported to Mayday, because he was by then a senior and didn't want to hear from the biddies, as he called them—the mutts, the twists, the hooters.

Mayday, by then, had dropped out of tenth, and was doing office work. Chick was in an "open" school—weaving, pottery, and group.

"How's your life going?" she asked him, the last time they had a real conversation.

"You're asking me how *my* life is?"

She didn't answer. She was vacuuming the rug, screaming over the noise.

He got up and turned the vacuum off. He looked at her—he was a foot taller, his grin wide, and stupid as ever. "You asking me?" he yelled.

"Yeah."

"It's fine," he said, pushing his face next to her face. She had on glasses but he could still get in there until his eyelashes brushed the lenses, his nose crushed into hers, their cheekbones grinding.

Then, crawling home one night—some kid had dropped him off in front of the old house, late and everyone asleep—he must have fainted, slipped, because the milkman found him there in a heap at six. All along there had been at least another one in there, or maybe the boozing had opened up an old one, and he bled to death on the porch, the house key in his hand.

When he got home, carrying a bag of groceries through the icy streets, the place was dark. Light from the hall fingered into the room, and his eyes followed the telephone cord to where she sat, an alley lamp lacing the window's frost. At first he thought, his eyes adjusting to the dark, that she was laughing.

"Can I turn a light on?" he asked, fumbling for the switch on the floor lamp, but by then he'd already skated on the beads—clear glass, fake pearl, wood; bean, ball and grain—causing them to spin across the floor. He had just that morning swept it clean of his rags and paper. He could still hear beads rolling. Months later they were still turning up in dust-balls, or nesting in the floorboards. Now his impulse was to get the dustpan and guide the beads to the middle where they could, at least, be seen. He mentioned the electric broom—long since sold—and how fast it could have eaten them. But still he hadn't moved. He stared at a spot beyond the lamplight where a pool of glass beads bathed in the window's frosty glare. He felt tired from the long day, yet resisted the impulse to sit down.

It was drafty by the window, and the bedsheets were icy, but her body was still heated from exertion. Only slowly had the dampness along her backbone, under her arms, and inside her shoes begun to dry. Soon she'd strip off the clammy things. She felt sick already, and yet too heavy and too tired to struggle.

First she eased off one shoe, then the other. It would take much effort, but next she would roll down and peel away the thick, damp socks. Then she'd stand—this was coming—and press under the pads of her soles and pink heels all this sharp sand. Was it sand or was it tapioca? She smiled. Tapioca was an old word for someone gone mental. The first time they heard it, they'd cracked up. Then they worked at it. The *thoughts* must be the tapioca, she said. Once hard and rustly like taps in the box, they turned to mush in the "yoka." Another way, he suggested—and already he was laughing—was a bad boy hit his head and underneath the crown: hot tapioca! Only this time, he said, call it tapioca-pudding. Their mother had heard enough, though, subject closed. But the subject stayed active; it was in their minds for months. If she but tapped her temple with a finger, he'd start laughing. That was the beauty of him. If you could find the spot, he could be reached. Flexing her toes, stiff with cold, she stood in the shadowy, moon-frosted room, and savored the sensation, like so many they shared, of things pressing into the flesh of the feet, making a map of red dots.

And so the long day of the call had already brought two comforts: first, the breaking of each necklace, the reel and reflux of the beads. Then— now—the prospect of walking that hard garden of seed.

Library of Congress Cataloging-in-Publication Data

McGarry, Jean.
    Home at last / Jean McGarry.
        p.   cm. — (Johns Hopkins, poetry and fiction)
      ISBN 0-8018-4852-0. — ISBN 0-8018-4853-9 (pbk.)
      I. Title. II. Series.
    PS3563.C3636H65   1994
    813'.54—dc20   93-45676